DOVER · THRIFT · EDITIONS

The Kreutzer Sonata and Other Short Stories

LEO TOLSTOY

DOVER PUBLICATIONS, INC.
New York

DOVER THRIFT EDITIONS

EDITOR: STANLEY APPELBAUM

Bibliographical Note

This Dover edition, first published in 1993,
is a new selection of three stories in English translation
reprinted from standard editions.
See the new "Note" opposite for further details.

Library of Congress Cataloging-in-Publication Data

Tolstoy, Leo, graf, 1828–1910.
[Short stories. English. Selections]
The Kreutzer sonata and other short stories / Leo Tolstoy.
p. cm. — (Dover thrift editions)
Contents: How much land does a man need? — The death of
Ivan Ilych — The Kreutzer sonata.
ISBN 0-486-27805-0 (pbk.)
1. Tolstoy, Leo, graf, 1828–1910—Translations into English.
I. Title. II. Series.
PG3366.A13 1993
891.73′3—dc20 93-35550
CIP

Manufactured in the United States of America
Dover Publications, Inc. 31 East 2nd Street, Mineola, N.Y. 11501

Note

THE WORLDWIDE FAME of Leo [Lev Nikolayevich] Tolstoy (1828–1910) rests largely on his two massive novels *War and Peace* (1865–69) and *Anna Karenina* (1875–77), but his short stories also form a highly significant part of his oeuvre. The three selected for the present volume were all written after his spiritual crisis of 1879, after which he preached a radical form of Christianity based closely on the original teachings of Christ himself.

"How Much Land Does a Man Need?" (1886) is one of Tolstoy's many simply written parables from this period concentrating on peasant life. "The Death of Ivan Ilych" (also 1886) is one of the author's most highly regarded works, a quest for the meaning of life and the proper way to live it. "The Kreutzer Sonata" (1891), probably Tolstoy's most notorious story, dealing as it does with jealousy and adultery, is also a serious condemnation of the mores and attitudes of the wealthy, educated class.

The translators of the first two stories, Louise and Aylmer Maude, indicated by acute accents the stressed syllables of the Russian proper names; in the present edition, these have been retained for only the first appearance of each name. (No attempt has been made to update whatever values of currency are mentioned.) The translator of "The Kreutzer Sonata" was uncredited in our source. The footnotes in square brackets were supplied by the present editor; the others, by the translators.

Contents

How Much Land Does a Man Need?

I

AN ELDER SISTER came to visit her younger sister in the country. The elder was married to a tradesman in town, the younger to a peasant in the village. As the sisters sat over their tea talking, the elder began to boast of the advantages of town life: saying how comfortably they lived there, how well they dressed, what fine clothes her children wore, what good things they ate and drank, and how she went to the theatre, promenades, and entertainments.

The younger sister was piqued, and in turn disparaged the life of a tradesman, and stood up for that of a peasant.

"I would not change my way of life for yours," said she. "We may live roughly, but at least we are free from anxiety. You live in better style than we do, but though you often earn more than you need, you are very likely to lose all you have. You know the proverb, 'Loss and gain are brothers twain.' It often happens that people who are wealthy one day are begging their bread the next. Our way is safer. Though a peasant's life is not a fat one, it is a long one. We shall never grow rich, but we shall always have enough to eat."

The elder sister said sneeringly:

"Enough? Yes, if you like to share with the pigs and the calves! What do you know of elegance or manners! However much your goodman may slave, you will die as you are living—on a dung heap—and your children the same."

"Well, what of that?" replied the younger. "Of course our work is rough and coarse. But, on the other hand, it is sure, and we need not bow to anyone. But you, in your towns, are surrounded by temptations; to-day all may be right, but to-morrow the Evil One may tempt your husband with cards, wine, or women, and all will go to ruin. Don't such things happen often enough?"

Pahóm, the master of the house, was lying on the top of the stove and he listened to the women's chatter.

"It is perfectly true," thought he. "Busy as we are from childhood tilling mother earth, we peasants have no time to let any nonsense settle in our heads. Our only trouble is that we haven't land enough. If I had plenty of land, I shouldn't fear the Devil himself!"

The women finished their tea, chatted a while about dress, and then cleared away the tea-things and lay down to sleep.

But the Devil had been sitting behind the stove, and had heard all that was said. He was pleased that the peasant's wife had led her husband into boasting, and that he had said that if he had plenty of land he would not fear the Devil himself.

"All right," thought the Devil. "We will have a tussle. I'll give you land enough; and by means of that land I will get you into my power."

II

Close to the village there lived a lady, a small landowner who had an estate of about three hundred acres.[1] She had always lived on good terms with the peasants until she engaged as her steward an old soldier, who took to burdening the people with fines. However careful Pahom tried to be, it happened again and again that now a horse of his got among the lady's oats, now a cow strayed into her garden, now his calves found their way into her meadows—and he always had to pay a fine.

Pahom paid up, but grumbled and, going home in a temper, was rough with his family. All through that summer, Pahom had much trouble because of this steward, and he was even glad when winter came and the cattle had to be stabled. Though he grudged the fodder when they could no longer graze on the pasture-land, at least he was free from anxiety about them.

In the winter the news got about that the lady was going to sell her land and that the keeper of the inn on the high road was bargaining for it. When the peasants heard this they were very much alarmed.

"Well," thought they, "if the innkeeper gets the land, he will worry us with fines worse than the lady's steward. We all depend on that estate."

So the peasants went on behalf of their Commune, and asked the lady not to sell the land to the innkeeper, offering her a better price for it themselves. The lady agreed to let them have it. Then the peasants tried to arrange for the Commune to buy the whole estate, so that it might be

[1] 120 desyatins. The desyatina is properly 2.7 acres; but in this story round numbers are used.

held by them all in common. They met twice to discuss it, but could not settle the matter; the Evil One sowed discord among them and they could not agree. So they decided to buy the land individually, each according to his means; and the lady agreed to this plan as she had to the other.

Presently Pahom heard that a neighbor of his was buying fifty acres, and that the lady had consented to accept one half in cash and to wait a year for the other half. Pahom felt envious.

"Look at that," thought he, "the land is all being sold, and I shall get none of it." So he spoke to his wife.

"Other people are buying," said he, "and we must also buy twenty acres or so. Life is becoming impossible. That steward is simply crushing us with his fines."

So they put their heads together and considered how they could manage to buy it. They had one hundred rubles laid by. They sold a colt and one half of their bees, hired out one of their sons as a laborer and took his wages in advance; borrowed the rest from a brother-in-law, and so scraped together half the purchase money.

Having done this, Pahom chose out a farm of forty acres, some of it wooded, and went to the lady to bargain for it. They came to an agreement, and he shook hands with her upon it and paid her a deposit in advance. Then they went to town and signed the deeds; he paying half the price down, and undertaking to pay the remainder within two years.

So now Pahom had land of his own. He borrowed seed, and sowed it on the land he had bought. The harvest was a good one, and within a year he had managed to pay off his debts both to the lady and to his brother-in-law. So he became a landowner, ploughing and sowing his own land, making hay on his own land, cutting his own trees, and feeding his cattle on his own pasture. When he went out to plough his fields, or to look at his growing corn, or at his grass-meadows, his heart would fill with joy. The grass that grew and the flowers that bloomed there seemed to him unlike any that grew elsewhere. Formerly, when he had passed by that land, it had appeared the same as any other land, but now it seemed quite different.

III

So Pahom was well-contented, and everything would have been right if the neighboring peasants would only not have trespassed on his corn-fields and meadows. He appealed to them most civilly, but they still went on: now the Communal herdsmen would let the village cows stray into his meadows, then horses from the night pasture would get among his corn. Pahom turned them out again and again, and forgave their owners, and for a long time he forbore to prosecute any one. But at last he lost patience and complained to the District Court. He knew it was the peasants' want of land, and no evil intent on their part, that caused the trouble, but he thought:

"I cannot go on overlooking it or they will destroy all I have. They must be taught a lesson."

So he had them up, gave them one lesson, and then another, and two or three of the peasants were fined. After a time Pahom's neighbors began to bear him a grudge for this, and would now and then let their cattle on to his land on purpose. One peasant even got into Pahom's wood at night and cut down five young lime trees for their bark. Pahom passing through the wood one day noticed something white. He came nearer and saw the stripped trunks lying on the ground, and close by stood the stumps where the trees had been. Pahom was furious.

"If he had only cut one here and there it would have been bad enough," thought Pahom, "but the rascal has actually cut down a whole clump. If I could only find out who did this, I would pay him out."

He racked his brain as to who it could be. Finally he decided: "It must be Simon—no one else could have done it." So he went to Simon's homestead to have a look round, but he found nothing, and only had an angry scene. However, he now felt more certain than ever that Simon had done it, and he lodged a complaint. Simon was summoned. The case was tried, and retried, and at the end of it all Simon was acquitted, there being no evidence against him. Pahom felt still more aggrieved, and let his anger loose upon the Elder and the Judges.

"You let thieves grease your palms," said he. "If you were honest folk yourselves you would not let a thief go free."

So Pahom quarrelled with the Judges and with his neighbors. Threats to burn his building began to be uttered. So though Pahom had more land, his place in the Commune was much worse than before.

About this time a rumor got about that many people were moving to new parts.

"There's no need for me to leave my land," thought Pahom. "But some of the others might leave our village and then there would be more room for us. I would take over their land myself and make my estate a bit bigger. I could then live more at ease. As it is, I am still too cramped to be comfortable."

One day Pahom was sitting at home when a peasant, passing through the village, happened to call in. He was allowed to stay the night, and supper was given him. Pahom had a talk with this peasant and asked him where he came from. The stranger answered that he came from beyond the Volga, where he had been working. One word led to another, and the man went on to say that many people were settling in those parts. He told how some people from his village had settled there. They had joined the Commune, and had had twenty-five acres per man granted them. The land was so good, he said, that the rye sown on it grew as high as a horse, and so thick that five cuts of a sickle made a sheaf. One peasant, he said, had brought nothing with him but his bare hands, and now he had six horses and two cows of his own.

Pahom's heart kindled with desire. He thought:

"Why should I suffer in this narrow hole, if one can live so well elsewhere? I will sell my land and my homestead here, and with the money I will start afresh over there and get everything new. In this crowded place one is always having trouble. But I must first go and find out all about it myself."

Towards summer he got ready and started. He went down the Volga on a steamer to Samara, then walked another three hundred miles on foot, and at last reached the place. It was just as the stranger had said. The peasants had plenty of land: every man had twenty-five acres of Communal land given him for his use, and any one who had money could buy, besides, at a ruble an acre as much good freehold land as he wanted.

Having found out all he wished to know, Pahom returned home as autumn came on, and began selling off his belongings. He sold his land at a profit, sold his homestead and all his cattle, and withdrew from membership in the Commune. He only waited till the spring, and then started with his family for the new settlement.

IV

As soon as Pahom and his family reached their new abode, he applied for admission into the Commune of a large village. He stood treat to the Elders and obtained the necessary documents. Five shares of Communal land were given him for his own and his sons' use: that is to say—125 acres (not all together, but in different fields) besides the use of the Communal pasture. Pahom put up the buildings he needed, and bought cattle. Of the Communal land alone he had three times as much as at his former home, and the land was good corn-land. He was ten times better off than he had been. He had plenty of arable land and pasturage, and could keep as many head of cattle as he liked.

At first, in the bustle of building and settling down, Pahom was pleased with it all, but when he got used to it he began to think that even here he had not enough land. The first year, he sowed wheat on his share of the Communal land and had a good crop. He wanted to go on sowing wheat, but had not enough Communal land for the purpose, and what he had already used was not available; for in those parts wheat is only sown on virgin soil or on fallow land. It is sown for one or two years, and then the land lies fallow till it is again overgrown with prairie grass. There were many who wanted such land and there was not enough for all; so that people quarreled about it. Those who were better off wanted it for growing wheat, and those who were poor wanted it to let to dealers, so that they might raise money to pay their taxes. Pahom wanted to sow more wheat, so he rented land from a dealer for a year. He sowed much wheat and had a fine crop, but the land was too far from the village—the wheat had to be carted more than ten miles. After a time Pahom noticed that some peasant-dealers were living on separate farms and were growing wealthy; and he thought:

"If I were to buy some freehold land and have a homestead on it, it would be a different thing altogether. Then it would all be nice and compact."

The question of buying freehold land recurred to him again and again.

He went on in the same way for three years, renting land and sowing wheat. The seasons turned out well and the crops were good, so that he began to lay money by. He might have gone on living contentedly, but he grew tired of having to rent other people's land every year, and having to scramble for it. Wherever there was good land to be had, the peasants would rush for it and it was taken up at once, so that unless you were sharp about it you got none. It happened in the third year that he and a dealer together rented a piece of pasture-land from some peasants; and they had already ploughed it up, when there was some dispute and the peasants went to law about it, and things fell out so that the labor was all lost.

"If it were my own land," thought Pahom, "I should be independent, and there would not be all this unpleasantness."

So Pahom began looking out for land which he could buy; and he came across a peasant who had bought thirteen hundred acres, but having got into difficulties was willing to sell again cheap. Pahom bargained and haggled with him, and at last they settled the price at 1,500 rubles, part in cash and part to be paid later. They had all but clinched the matter when a passing dealer happened to stop at Pahom's one day to get a feed for his horses. He drank tea with Pahom and they had a talk. The dealer said that he was just returning from the land of the Bashkirs,[1] far away, where he had bought thirteen thousand acres of land, all for 1,000 rubles. Pahom questioned him further, and the tradesman said:

"All one need do is to make friends with the chiefs. I gave away about one hundred rubles' worth of silk robes and carpets, besides a case of tea, and I gave wine to those who would drink it; and I got the land for less than a penny an acre."[2] And he showed Pahom the title-deeds, saying:

"The land lies near a river, and the whole prairie is virgin soil."

Pahom plied him with questions, and the tradesman said:

"There is more land there than you could cover if you walked a year, and it all belongs to the Bashkirs. They are as simple as sheep, and land can be got almost for nothing."

"There now," thought Pahom, "with my one thousand rubles, why should I get only thirteen hundred acres, and saddle myself with a debt besides? If I take it out there, I can get more than ten times as much for the money."

V

Pahom inquired how to get to the place, and as soon as the tradesman had left him, he prepared to go there himself. He left his wife to look after the homestead, and started on his journey taking his man with him. They stopped at a town on their way and bought a case of tea, some wine, and other presents, as the tradesman had advised. On and on they went until they had gone more than three hundred miles, and on the seventh day they came to a place where the Bashkirs had pitched their tents. It was all just as the tradesman had said. The people lived on the steppes, by a river, in felt-covered tents.[3] They neither tilled the ground, nor ate bread. Their cattle and horses grazed in herds on the steppe. The colts were tethered behind the tents, and the mares were driven to them twice a day.

[1] [Turkic people dwelling on both sides of the Urals.]

[2] Five kopeks for a desyatina.

[3] A kibitka is a movable dwelling, made up of detachable wooden frames, forming a round, and covered over with felt.

The mares were milked, and from the milk kumiss[1] was made. It was the women who prepared kumiss, and they also made cheese. As far as the men were concerned, drinking kumiss and tea, eating mutton, and playing on their pipes, was all they cared about. They were all stout and merry, and all the summer long they never thought of doing any work. They were quite ignorant, and knew no Russian, but were good-natured enough.

As soon as they saw Pahom, they came out of their tents and gathered round their visitor. An interpreter was found, and Pahom told them he had come about some land. The Bashkirs seemed very glad; they took Pahom and led him into one of the best tents, where they made him sit on some down cushions placed on a carpet, while they sat round him. They gave him some tea and kumiss, and had a sheep killed, and gave him mutton to eat. Pahom took presents out of his cart and distributed them among the Bashkirs, and divided the tea amongst them. The Bashkirs were delighted. They talked a great deal among themselves, and then told the interpreter to translate.

"They wish to tell you," said the interpreter, "that they like you, and that it is our custom to do all we can to please a guest and to repay him for his gifts. You have given us presents, now tell us which of the things we possess please you best, that we may present them to you."

"What pleases me best here," answered Pahom, "is your land. Our land is crowded and the soil is exhausted; but you have plenty of land and it is good land. I never saw the like of it."

The interpreter translated. The Bashkirs talked among themselves for a while. Pahom could not understand what they were saying, but saw that they were much amused and that they shouted and laughed. Then they were silent and looked at Pahom while the interpreter said:

"They wish me to tell you that in return for your presents they will gladly give you as much land as you want. You have only to point it out with your hand and it is yours."

The Bashkirs talked again for a while and began to dispute. Pahom asked what they were disputing about, and the interpreter told him that some of them thought they ought to ask their Chief about the land and not act in his absence, while others thought there was no need to wait for his return.

[1] [A fermented drink.]

VI

While the Bashkirs were disputing, a man in a large fox-fur cap appeared on the scene. They all became silent and rose to their feet. The interpreter said, "This is our Chief himself."

Pahom immediately fetched the best dressing-gown and five pounds of tea, and offered these to the Chief. The Chief accepted them, and seated himself in the place of honor. The Bashkirs at once began telling him something. The Chief listened for a while, then made a sign with his head for them to be silent, and addressing himself to Pahom, said in Russian:

"Well, let it be so. Choose whatever piece of land you like; we have plenty of it."

"How can I take as much as I like?" thought Pahom. "I must get a deed to make it secure, or else they may say, 'It is yours,' and afterwards may take it away again."

"Thank you for your kind words," he said aloud. "You have much land, and I only want a little. But I should like to be sure which bit is mine. Could it not be measured and made over to me? Life and death are in God's hands. You good people give it to me, but your children might wish to take it away again."

"You are quite right," said the Chief. "We will make it over to you."

"I heard that a dealer had been here," continued Pahom, "and that you gave him a little land, too, and signed title-deeds to that effect. I should like to have it done in the same way."

The Chief understood.

"Yes," replied he, "that can be done quite easily. We have a scribe, and we will go to town with you and have the deed properly sealed."

"And what will be the price?" asked Pahom.

"Our price is always the same: one thousand rubles a day."

Pahom did not understand.

"A day? What measure is that? How many acres would that be?"

"We do not know how to reckon it out," said the Chief. "We sell it by the day. As much as you can go round on your feet in a day is yours, and the price is one thousand rubles a day."

Pahom was surprised.

"But in a day you can get round a large tract of land," he said.

The Chief laughed.

"It will all be yours!" said he. "But there is one condition: If you don't return on the same day to the spot whence you started, your money is lost."

"But how am I to mark the way that I have gone?"

"Why, we shall go to any spot you like, and stay there. You must start from that spot and make your round, taking a spade with you. Wherever you think necessary, make a mark. At every turning, dig a hole and pile up the turf; then afterwards we will go round with a plough from hole to hole. You may make as large a circuit as you please, but before the sun sets you must return to the place you started from. All the land you cover will be yours."

Pahom was delighted. It was decided to start early next morning. They talked a while, and after drinking some more kumiss and eating some more mutton, they had tea again, and then the night came on. They gave Pahom a feather-bed to sleep on, and the Bashkirs dispersed for the night, promising to assemble the next morning at daybreak and ride out before sunrise to the appointed spot.

VII

Pahom lay on the feather-bed, but could not sleep. He kept thinking about the land.

"What a large tract I will mark off!" thought he. "I can easily do thirty-five miles in a day. The days are long now, and within a circuit of thirty-five miles what a lot of land there will be! I will sell the poorer land, or let it to peasants, but I'll pick out the best and farm it. I will buy two oxteams, and hire two more laborers. About a hundred and fifty acres shall be plough-land, and I will pasture cattle on the rest."

Pahom lay awake all night, and dozed off only just before dawn. Hardly were his eyes closed when he had a dream. He thought he was lying in that same tent and heard somebody chuckling outside. He wondered who it could be, and rose and went out, and he saw the Bashkir Chief sitting in front of the tent holding his sides and rolling about with laughter. Going nearer to the Chief, Pahom asked: "What are you laughing at?" But he saw that it was no longer the Chief, but the dealer who had recently stopped at his house and had told him about the land. Just as Pahom was going to ask, "Have you been here long?" he saw that it was not the dealer, but the peasant who had come up from the Volga, long ago, to Pahom's old home. Then he saw that it was not the peasant either, but the Devil himself with hoofs and horns, sitting there and chuckling, and before him lay a man barefoot, prostrate on the ground, with only trousers and a shirt on. And Pahom dreamt that he looked more attentively to see what sort of a man it was that was lying there, and he saw that the man was dead, and that it was himself! He awoke horror-struck.

"What things one does dream," thought he.

Looking round he saw through the open door that the dawn was breaking.

"It's time to wake them up," thought he. "We ought to be starting."

He got up, roused his man (who was sleeping in his cart), bade him harness; and went to call the Bashkirs.

"It's time to go to the steppe to measure the land," he said.

The Bashkirs rose and assembled, and the Chief came too. Then they began drinking kumiss again, and offered Pahom some tea, but he would not wait.

"If we are to go, let us go. It is high time," said he.

VIII

The Bashkirs got ready and they all started: some mounted on horses, and some in carts. Pahom drove in his own small cart with his servant and took a spade with him. When they reached the steppe, the morning red was beginning to kindle. They ascended a hillock (called by the Bashkirs a *shikhan*) and dismounting from their carts and their horses, gathered in one spot. The Chief came up to Pahom and stretching out his arm towards the plain:

"See," said he, "all this, as far as your eye can reach, is ours. You may have any part of it you like."

Pahom's eyes glistened: it was all virgin soil, as flat as the palm of your hand, as black as the seed of a poppy, and in the hollows different kinds of grasses grew breast high.

The Chief took off his fox-fur cap, placed it on the ground and said:

"This will be the mark. Start from here, and return here again. All the land you go round shall be yours."

Pahom took out his money and put it on the cap. Then he took off his outer coat, remaining in his sleeveless under-coat. He unfastened his girdle and tied it tight below his stomach, put a little bag of bread into the breast of his coat, and tying a flask of water to his girdle, he drew up the tops of his boots, took the spade from his man, and stood ready to start. He considered for some moments which way he had better go—it was tempting everywhere.

"No matter," he concluded, "I will go towards the rising sun."

He turned his face to the east, stretched himself, and waited for the sun to appear above the rim.

"I must lose no time," he thought, "and it is easier walking while it is still cool."

The sun's rays had hardly flashed above the horizon, before Pahom, carrying the spade over his shoulder, went down into the steppe.

Pahom started walking neither slowly nor quickly. After having gone a thousand yards he stopped, dug a hole, and placed pieces of turf one on another to make it more visible. Then he went on; and now that he had walked off his stiffness he quickened his pace. After a while he dug another hole.

Pahom looked back. The hillock could be distinctly seen in the sunlight, with the people on it, and the glittering tires of the cart-wheels. At a rough guess Pahom concluded that he had walked three miles. It was growing warmer; he took off his under-coat, flung it across his shoulder, and went on again. It had grown quite warm now; he looked at the sun, it was time to think of breakfast.

"The first shift is done, but there are four in a day, and it is too soon yet to turn. But I will just take off my boots," said he to himself.

He sat down, took off his boots, stuck them into his girdle, and went on. It was easy walking now.

"I will go on for another three miles," thought he, "and then turn to the left. This spot is so fine, that it would be a pity to lose it. The further one goes, the better the land seems."

He went straight on for a while, and when he looked round, the hillock was scarcely visible and the people on it looked like black ants, and he could just see something glistening there in the sun.

"Ah," thought Pahom, "I have gone far enough in this direction, it is time to turn. Besides I am in a regular sweat, and very thirsty."

He stopped, dug a large hole, and heaped up pieces of turf. Next he untied his flask, had a drink, and then turned sharply to the left. He went on and on; the grass was high, and it was very hot.

Pahom began to grow tired: he looked at the sun and saw that it was noon.

"Well," he thought, "I must have a rest."

He sat down, and ate some bread and drank some water; but he did not lie down, thinking that if he did he might fall asleep. After sitting a little while, he went on again. At first he walked easily: the food had strengthened him; but it had become terribly hot and he felt sleepy, still he went on, thinking: "An hour to suffer, a life-time to live."

He went a long way in this direction also, and was about to turn to the left again, when he perceived a damp hollow: "It would be a pity to leave that out," he thought. "Flax would do well there." So he went on past the hollow, and dug a hole on the other side of it before he turned the corner. Pahom looked towards the hillock. The heat made the air hazy: it seemed to be quivering, and through the haze the people on the hillock could scarcely be seen.

"Ah!" thought Pahom, "I have made the sides too long; I must make this one shorter." And he went along the third side, stepping faster. He looked at the sun: it was nearly half-way to the horizon, and he had not yet done two miles of the third side of the square. He was still ten miles from the goal.

"No," he thought, "though it will make my land lop-sided, I must hurry back in a straight line now. I might go too far, and as it is I have a great deal of land."

So Pahom hurriedly dug a hole, and turned straight towards the hillock.

IX

Pahom went straight towards the hillock, but he now walked with difficulty. He was done up with the heat, his bare feet were cut and bruised, and his legs began to fail. He longed to rest, but it was impossible if he meant to get back before sunset. The sun waits for no man, and it was sinking lower and lower.

"Oh dear," he thought, "if only I have not blundered trying for too much! What if I am too late?"

He looked towards the hillock and at the sun. He was still far from his goal, and the sun was already near the rim.

Pahom walked on and on; it was very hard walking but he went quicker and quicker. He pressed on, but was still far from the place. He began running, threw away his coat, his boots, his flask, and his cap, and kept only the spade which he used as a support.

"What shall I do," he thought again, "I have grasped too much and ruined the whole affair. I can't get there before the sun sets."

And this fear made him still more breathless. Pahom went on running, his soaking shirt and trousers stuck to him and his mouth was parched. His breast was working like a blacksmith's bellows, his heart was beating like a hammer, and his legs were giving way as if they did not belong to him. Pahom was seized with terror lest he should die of the strain.

Though afraid of death, he could not stop. "After having run all that way they will call me a fool if I stop now," thought he. And he ran on and on, and drew near and heard the Bashkirs yelling and shouting to him, and their cries inflamed his heart still more. He gathered his last strength and ran on.

The sun was close to the rim, and cloaked in mist looked large, and red as blood. Now, yes now, it was about to set! The sun was quite low, but he was also quite near his aim. Pahom could already see the people on the hillock waving their arms to hurry him up. He could see the fox-fur cap on the ground and the money on it, and the Chief sitting on the ground holding his sides. And Pahom remembered his dream.

"There is plenty of land," thought he, "but will God let me live on it? I have lost my life, I have lost my life! I shall never reach that spot!"

Pahom looked at the sun, which had reached the earth: one side of it had already disappeared. With all his remaining strength he rushed on, bending his body forward so that his legs could hardly follow fast enough to keep him from falling. Just as he reached the hillock it suddenly grew dark. He looked up—the sun had already set! He gave a cry: "All my labor has been in vain," thought he, and was about to stop, but he heard the Bashkirs still shouting, and remembered that though to him, from below, the sun seemed to have set, they on the hillock could still see it. He took a long breath and ran up the hillock. It was still light there. He reached the top and saw the cap. Before it sat the Chief laughing and holding his sides. Again Pahom remembered his dream, and he uttered a cry: his legs gave way beneath him, he fell forward and reached the cap with his hands.

"Ah, that's a fine fellow!" exclaimed the Chief. "He has gained much land!"

Pahom's servant came running up and tried to raise him, but he saw that blood was flowing from his mouth. Pahom was dead!

The Bashkirs clicked their tongues to show their pity.

His servant picked up the spade and dug a grave long enough for Pahom to lie in, and buried him in it. Six feet from his head to his heels was all he needed.

The Death of Ivan Ilych

I

DURING AN INTERVAL in the Melvínski trial in the large building of the Law Courts the members and public prosecutor met in Iván Egórovich Shébek's private room, where the conversation turned on the celebrated Krasóvski case. Fëdor Vasílievich warmly maintained that it was not subject to their jurisdiction, Ivan Egorovich maintained the contrary, while Peter Ivánovich, not having entered into the discussion at the start, took no part in it but looked through the *Gazette* which had just been handed in.

"Gentlemen," he said, "Iván Ilých has died!"

"You don't say so!"

"Here, read it yourself," replied Peter Ivanovich, handing Fedor Vasilievich the paper still damp from the press. Surrounded by a black border were the words: "Praskóvya Fëdorovna Goloviná, with profound sorrow, informs relatives and friends of the demise of her beloved husband Ivan Ilych Golovín, Member of the Court of Justice, which occurred on February the 4th of this year 1882. The funeral will take place on Friday at one o'clock in the afternoon."

Ivan Ilych had been a colleague of the gentlemen present and was liked by them all. He had been ill for some weeks with an illness said to be incurable. His post had been kept open for him, but there had been conjectures that in case of his death Alexéev might receive his appointment, and that either Vínnikov or Shtábel would succeed Alexeev. So on receiving the news of Ivan Ilych's death the first thought of each of the gentlemen in that private room was of the changes and promotions it might occasion among themselves or their acquaintances.

"I shall be sure to get Shtabel's place or Vinnikov's," thought Fedor Vasilievich. "I was promised that long ago, and the promotion means an extra eight hundred rubles a year for me besides the allowance."

"Now I must apply for my brother-in-law's transfer from Kaluga," thought Peter Ivanovich. "My wife will be very glad, and then she won't be able to say that I never do anything for her relations."

"I thought he would never leave his bed again," said Peter Ivanovich aloud. "It's very sad."

"But what really was the matter with him?"

"The doctors couldn't say—at least they could, but each of them said something different. When last I saw him I thought he was getting better."

"And I haven't been to see him since the holidays. I always meant to go."

"Had he any property?"

"I think his wife had a little—but something quite trifling."

"We shall have to go to see her, but they live so terribly far away."

"Far away from you, you mean. Everything's far away from your place."

"You see, he never can forgive my living on the other side of the river," said Peter Ivanovich, smiling at Shebek. Then, still talking of the distances between different parts of the city, they returned to the Court.

Besides considerations as to the possible transfers and promotions likely to result from Ivan Ilych's death, the mere fact of the death of a near acquaintance aroused, as usual, in all who heard of it the complacent feeling that "it is he who is dead and not I."

Each one thought or felt, "Well, he's dead but I'm alive!" But the more intimate of Ivan Ilych's acquaintances, his so-called friends, could not help thinking also that they would now have to fulfil the very tiresome demands of propriety by attending the funeral service and paying a visit of condolence to the widow.

Fedor Vasilievich and Peter Ivanovich had been his nearest acquaintances. Peter Ivanovich had studied law with Ivan Ilych and had considered himself to be under obligations to him.

Having told his wife at dinner-time of Ivan Ilych's death, and of his conjecture that it might be possible to get her brother transferred to their circuit, Peter Ivanovich sacrificed his usual nap, put on his evening clothes, and drove to Ivan Ilych's house.

At the entrance stood a carriage and two cabs. Leaning against the wall in the hall downstairs near the cloak-stand was a coffin-lid covered with cloth of gold, ornamented with gold cord and tassels, that had been polished up with metal powder. Two ladies in black were taking off their fur cloaks. Peter Ivanovich recognized one of them as Ivan Ilych's sister, but the other was a stranger to him. His colleague Schwartz was just coming downstairs, but on seeing Peter Ivanovich enter he stopped and winked at him, as if to say: "Ivan Ilych has made a mess of things—not like you and me."

Schwartz's face with his Piccadilly whiskers, and his slim figure in evening dress, had as usual an air of elegant solemnity which contrasted with the playfulness of his character and had a special piquancy here, or so it seemed to Peter Ivanovich.

Peter Ivanovich allowed the ladies to precede him and slowly followed them upstairs. Schwartz did not come down but remained where he was, and Peter Ivanovich understood that he wanted to arrange where they should play bridge that evening. The ladies went upstairs to the widow's room, and Schwartz with seriously compressed lips but a playful look in his eyes, indicated by a twist of his eyebrows the room to the right where the body lay.

Peter Ivanovich, like everyone else on such occasions, entered feeling uncertain what he would have to do. All he knew was that at such times it is always safe to cross oneself. But he was not quite sure whether one should make obeisances while doing so. He therefore adopted a middle course. On entering the room he began crossing himself and made a slight movement resembling a bow. At the same time, as far as the motion of his head and arm allowed, he surveyed the room. Two young men—apparently nephews, one of whom was a high-school pupil—were leaving the room, crossing themselves as they did so. An old woman was standing motionless, and a lady with strangely arched eyebrows was saying something to her in a whisper. A vigorous, resolute Church Reader, in a frock-coat, was reading something in a loud voice with an expression that precluded any contradiction. The butler's assistant, Gerásim, stepping lightly in front of Peter Ivanovich, was strewing something on the floor. Noticing this, Peter Ivanovich was immediately aware of a faint odour of a decomposing body.

The last time he had called on Ivan Ilych, Peter Ivanovich had seen Gerasim in the study. Ivan Ilych had been particularly fond of him and he was performing the duty of a sick nurse.

Peter Ivanovich continued to make a sign of the cross slightly inclining his head in an intermediate direction between the coffin, the Reader, and the icons on the table in a corner of the room. Afterwards, when it seemed to him that this movement of his arm in crossing himself had gone on too long, he stopped and began to look at the corpse.

The dead man lay, as dead men always lie, in a specially heavy way, his rigid limbs sunk in the soft cushions of the coffin, with the head forever bowed on the pillow. His yellow waxen brow with bald patches over his sunken temples was thrust up in the way peculiar to the dead, the protruding nose seeming to press on the upper lip. He was much changed and had grown even thinner since Peter Ivanovich had last seen him, but, as is always the case with the dead, his face was handsomer and above all more dignified than when he was alive. The expression on the face said that what was necessary had been accomplished, and accomplished rightly. Besides this there was in that expression a reproach and a warning to the living. This warning seemed to Peter Ivanovich out of place, or at least not applicable to him. He felt a certain discomfort and so he hurriedly crossed himself once more and turned and went out of the door—too hurriedly and too regardless of propriety, as he himself was aware.

Schwartz was waiting for him in the adjoining room with legs spread wide apart and both hands toying with his top-hat behind his back. The mere sight of that playful, well-groomed, and elegant figure refreshed Peter Ivanovich. He felt that Schwartz was above all these happenings and would not surrender to any depressing influences. His very look said that this incident of a church service for Ivan Ilych could not be a sufficient reason for infringing the order of the session—in other words, that it would certainly not prevent his unwrapping a new pack of cards and shuffling them that evening while a footman placed four fresh candles on the table: in fact, that there was no reason for supposing that this incident would hinder their spending the evening agreeably. Indeed he said this in a whisper as Peter Ivanovich passed him, proposing that they should meet for a game at Fedor Vasilievich's. But apparently Peter Ivanovich was not destined to play bridge that evening. Praskovya Fedorovna (a short, fat woman who despite all efforts to the contrary had continued to broaden steadily from her shoulders downwards and who had the same extraordinarily arched eyebrows as the lady who had been standing by the coffin), dressed all in black, her head covered with lace, came out of her own room with some other ladies, conducted them to the room where the dead body lay, and said: "The service will begin immediately. Please go in."

Schwartz, making an indefinite bow, stood still, evidently neither accepting nor declining this invitation. Praskovya Fedorovna, recognizing Peter Ivanovich, sighed, went close up to him, took his hand, and said: "I know you were a true friend to Ivan Ilych . . ." and looked at him awaiting some suitable response. And Peter Ivanovich knew that, just as it had been the right thing to cross himself in that room, so what he had to do here was to press her hand, sigh, and say, "Believe me. . . ." So he did all this and as he did it felt that the desired result had been achieved: that both he and she were touched.

"Come with me. I want to speak to you before it begins," said the widow. "Give me your arm."

Peter Ivanovich gave her his arm and they went to the inner rooms, passing Schwartz who winked at Peter Ivanovich compassionately.

"That does for our bridge! Don't object if we find another player. Perhaps you can cut in when you do escape," said his playful look.

Peter Ivanovich sighed still more deeply and despondently, and Praskovya Fedorovna pressed his arm gratefully. When they reached the drawing-room, upholstered in pink cretonne and lighted by a dim lamp, they sat down at the table—she on a sofa and Peter Ivanovich on a low pouffe, the springs of which yielded spasmodically under his weight. Praskovya Fedorovna had been on the point of warning him to take another seat, but felt that such a warning was out of keeping with her present condition and so changed her mind. As he sat down on the pouffe Peter Ivanovich recalled how Ivan Ilych had arranged this room and had consulted him regarding this pink cretonne with green leaves. The whole room was full of furniture and knick-knacks, and on her way to the sofa the lace of the widow's black shawl caught on the carved edge of the table. Peter Ivanovich rose to detach it, and the springs of the pouffe, relieved of his weight, rose also and gave him a push. The widow began detaching her shawl herself, and Peter Ivanovich again sat down, suppressing the rebellious springs of the pouffe under him. But the widow had not quite freed herself and Peter Ivanovich got up again, and again the pouffe rebelled and even creaked. When this was all over she took out a clean cambric handkerchief and began to weep. The episode with the shawl and the struggle with the pouffe had cooled Peter Ivanovich's emotions and he sat there with a sullen look on his face. This awkward situation was interrupted by Sokolóv, Ivan Ilych's butler, who came to report that the plot in the cemetery that Praskovya Fedorovna had chosen would cost two hundred rubles. She stopped weeping and, looking at Peter Ivanovich with the air of a victim, remarked in French that it was very hard for her. Peter Ivanovich made a silent gesture signifying his full conviction that it must indeed be so.

"Please smoke," she said in a magnanimous yet crushed voice, and turned to discuss with Sokolov the price of the plot for the grave.

Peter Ivanovich while lighting his cigarette heard her inquiring very circumstantially into the prices of different plots in the cemetery and finally decide which she would take. When that was done she gave instructions about engaging the choir. Sokolov then left the room.

"I look after everything myself," she told Peter Ivanovich, shifting the albums that lay on the table; and noticing that the table was endangered by his cigarette-ash, she immediately passed him an ash-tray, saying as she did so: "I consider it an affectation to say that my grief prevents my attending to practical affairs. On the contrary, if anything can—I won't say console me, but—distract me, it is seeing to everything concerning him." She again took out her handkerchief as if preparing to cry, but suddenly, as if mastering her feeling, she shook herself and began to speak calmly. "But there is something I want to talk to you about."

Peter Ivanovich bowed, keeping control of the springs of the pouffe, which immediately began quivering under him.

"He suffered terribly the last few days."

"Did he?" said Peter Ivanovich.

"Oh, terribly! He screamed unceasingly, not for minutes but for hours. For the last three days he screamed incessantly. It was unendurable. I cannot understand how I bore it; you could hear him three rooms off. Oh, what I have suffered!"

"Is it possible that he was conscious all that time?" asked Peter Ivanovich.

"Yes," she whispered. "To the last moment. He took leave of us a quarter of an hour before he died, and asked us to take Volódya away."

The thought of the sufferings of this man he had known so intimately, first as a merry little boy, then as a school-mate, and later as a grown-up colleague, suddenly struck Peter Ivanovich with horror, despite an unpleasant consciousness of his own and this woman's dissimulation. He again saw that brow, and that nose pressing down on the lip, and felt afraid for himself.

"Three days of frightful suffering and then death! Why, that might suddenly, at any time, happen to me," he thought, and for a moment felt terrified. But—he did not himself know how—the customary reflection at once occurred to him that this had happened to Ivan Ilych and not to him, and that it should not and could not happen to him, and that to think that it could would be yielding to depression which he ought not to do, as Schwartz's expression plainly showed. After which reflection Peter Ivanovich felt reassured, and began to ask with interest about the details of Ivan Ilych's death, as though death was an accident natural to Ivan Ilych but certainly not to himself.

After many details of the really dreadful physical sufferings Ivan Ilych had endured (which details he learnt only from the effect those sufferings had produced on Praskovya Fedorovna's nerves) the widow apparently found it necessary to get to business.

"Oh, Peter Ivanovich, how hard it is! How terribly, terribly hard!" and she again began to weep.

Peter Ivanovich sighed and waited for her to finish blowing her nose. When she had done so he said, "Believe me . . . ," and she again began talking and brought out what was evidently her chief concern with him—

namely, to question him as to how she could obtain a grant of money from the government on the occasion of her husband's death. She made it appear that she was asking Peter Ivanovich's advice about her pension, but he soon saw that she already knew about that to the minutest detail, more even than he did himself. She knew how much could be got out of the government in consequence of her husband's death, but wanted to find out whether she could not possibly extract something more. Peter Ivanovich tried to think of some means of doing so, but after reflecting for a while and, out of propriety, condemning the government for its niggardliness, he said he thought that nothing more could be got. Then she sighed and evidently began to devise means of getting rid of her visitor. Noticing this, he put out his cigarette, rose, pressed her hand, and went out into the anteroom.

In the dining-room where the clock stood that Ivan Ilych had liked so much and had bought at an antique shop, Peter Ivanovich met a priest and a few acquaintances who had come to attend the service, and he recognized Ivan Ilych's daughter, a handsome young woman. She was in black and her slim figure appeared slimmer than ever. She had a gloomy, determined, almost angry expression, and bowed to Peter Ivanovich as though he were in some way to blame. Behind her, with the same offended look, stood a wealthy young man, an examining magistrate, whom Peter Ivanovich also knew and who was her fiancé, as he had heard. He bowed mournfully to them and was about to pass into the death-chamber, when from under the stairs appeared the figure of Ivan Ilych's schoolboy son, who was extremely like his father. He seemed a little Ivan Ilych, such as Peter Ivanovich remembered when they studied law together. His tear-stained eyes had in them the look that is seen in the eyes of boys of thirteen or fourteen who are not pure-minded. When he saw Peter Ivanovich he scowled morosely and shamefacedly. Peter Ivanovich nodded to him and entered the death-chamber. The service began: candles, groans, incense, tears, and sobs. Peter Ivanovich stood looking gloomily down at his feet. He did not look once at the dead man, did not yield to any depressing influence, and was one of the first to leave the room. There was no one in the anteroom, but Gerasim darted out of the dead man's room, rummaged with his strong hands among the fur coats to find Peter Ivanovich's and helped him on with it.

"Well, friend Gerasim," said Peter Ivanovich, so as to say something. "It's a sad affair, isn't it?"

"It's God's will. We shall all come to it some day," said Gerasim, displaying his teeth—the even, white teeth of a healthy peasant—and, like a man in the thick of urgent work, he briskly opened the front door, called the coachman, helped Peter Ivanovich into the sledge, and sprang back to the porch as if in readiness for what he had to do next.

Peter Ivanovich found the fresh air particularly pleasant after the smell of incense, the dead body, and carbolic acid.

"Where to, sir?" asked the coachman.

"It's not too late even now. . . . I'll call round on Fedor Vasilievich."

He accordingly drove there and found them just finishing the first rubber, so that it was quite convenient for him to cut in.

II

Ivan Ilych's life had been most simple and most ordinary and therefore most terrible.

He had been a member of the Court of Justice, and died at the age of forty-five. His father had been an official who after serving in various ministries and departments in Petersburg had made the sort of career which brings men to positions from which by reason of their long service they cannot be dismissed, though they are obviously unfit to hold any responsible position, and for whom therefore posts are specially created, which though fictitious carry salaries of from six to ten thousand rubles that are not fictitious, and in receipt of which they live on to a great age.

Such was the Privy Councillor and superfluous member of various superfluous institutions, Ilyá Epímovich Golovin.

He had three sons, of whom Ivan Ilych was the second. The eldest son was following in his father's footsteps only in another department, and was already approaching that stage in the service at which a similar sinecure would be reached. The third son was a failure. He had ruined his prospects in a number of positions and was now serving in the railway department. His father and brothers, and still more their wives, not merely disliked meeting him, but avoided remembering his existence unless compelled to do so. His sister had married Baron Greff, a Petersburg official of her father's type. Ivan Ilych was *le phénix de la famille*[1] as people said. He was neither as cold and formal as his elder brother nor as wild as the younger, but was a happy mean between them—an intelligent, polished, lively and agreeable man. He had studied with his younger brother at the School of Law, but the latter had failed to complete

[1] [The phoenix of the family.]

the course and was expelled when he was in the fifth class. Ivan Ilych finished the course well. Even when he was at the School of Law he was just what he remained for the rest of his life: a capable, cheerful, good-natured, and sociable man, though strict in the fulfillment of what he considered to be his duty: and he considered his duty to be what was so considered by those in authority. Neither as a boy nor as a man was he a toady, but from early youth was by nature attracted to people of high station as a fly is drawn to the light, assimilating their ways and views of life and establishing friendly relations with them. All the enthusiasms of childhood and youth passed without leaving much trace on him; he succumbed to sensuality, to vanity, and latterly among the highest classes to liberalism, but always within limits which his instinct unfailingly indicated to him as correct.

At school he had done things which had formerly seemed to him very horrid and made him feel disgusted with himself when he did them; but when later on he saw that such actions were done by people of good position and that they did not regard them as wrong, he was able not exactly to regard them as right, but to forget about them entirely or not be at all troubled at remembering them.

Having graduated from the School of Law and qualified for the tenth rank of the civil service, and having received money from his father for his equipment, Ivan Ilych ordered himself clothes at Scharmer's, the fashionable tailor, hung a medallion inscribed *respice finem*[1] on his watch-chain, took leave of his professor and the prince who was patron of the school, had a farewell dinner with his comrades at Donon's first-class restaurant, and with his new and fashionable portmanteau, linen, clothes, shaving and other toilet appliances, and a travelling rug, all purchased at the best shops, he set off for one of the provinces where, through his father's influence, he had been attached to the Governor as an official for special service.

In the province Ivan Ilych soon arranged as easy and agreeable a position for himself as he had had at the School of Law. He performed his official tasks, made his career, and at the same time amused himself pleasantly and decorously. Occasionally he paid official visits to country districts, where he behaved with dignity both to his superiors and inferiors, and performed the duties entrusted to him, which related chiefly to the sectarians, with an exactness and incorruptible honesty of which he could not but feel proud.

In official matters, despite his youth and taste for frivolous gaiety, he

[1] [Consider the end.]

was exceedingly reserved, punctilious, and even severe; but in society he was often amusing and witty, and always good-natured, correct in his manner, and *bon enfant*,[1] as the governor and his wife—with whom he was like one of the family—used to say of him.

In the province he had an affair with a lady who made advances to the elegant young lawyer, and there was also a milliner; and there were carousals with aides-de-camp who visited the district, and after-supper visits to a certain outlying street of doubtful reputation; and there was too some obsequiousness to his chief and even to his chief's wife, but all this was done with such a tone of good breeding that no hard names could be applied to it. It all came under the heading of the French saying: "*Il faut que jeunesse se passe.*"[2] It was all done with clean hands, in clean linen, with French phrases, and above all among people of the best society and consequently with the approval of people of rank.

So Ivan Ilych served for five years and then came a change in his official life. The new and reformed judicial institutions were introduced, and new men were needed. Ivan Ilych became such a new man. He was offered the post of Examining Magistrate, and he accepted it though the post was in another province and obliged him to give up the connexions he had formed and to make new ones. His friends met to give him a send-off; they had a group-photograph taken and presented him with a silver cigarette-case, and he set off to his new post.

As examining magistrate Ivan Ilych was just as *comme il faut*[3] and decorous a man, inspiring general respect and capable of separating his official duties from his private life, as he had been when acting as an official on special service. His duties now as examining magistrate were far more interesting and attractive than before. In his former position it had been pleasant to wear an undress uniform made by Scharmer, and to pass through the crowd of petitioners and officials who were timorously awaiting an audience with the governor, and who envied him as with free and easy gait he went straight into his chief's private room to have a cup of tea and a cigarette with him. But not many people had then been directly dependent on him—only police officials and the sectarians when he went on special missions—and he liked to treat them politely, almost as comrades, as if he were letting them feel that he who had the power to crush them was treating them in this simple, friendly way. There were then but few such people. But now, as an examining magistrate, Ivan Ilych felt that everyone without exception, even the most important and

[1] [Good sort, cheerful companion.]
[2] Youth must have its fling.
[3] [Proper.]

self-satisfied, was in his power, and that he need only write a few words on a sheet of paper with a certain heading, and this or that important, self-satisfied person would be brought before him in the role of an accused person or a witness, and if he did not choose to allow him to sit down, would have to stand before him and answer his questions. Ivan Ilych never abused his power; he tried on the contrary to soften its expression, but the consciousness of it and of the possibility of softening its effect, supplied the chief interest and attraction of his office. In his work itself, especially in his examinations, he very soon acquired a method of eliminating all considerations irrelevant to the legal aspect of the case, and reducing even the most complicated case to a form in which it would be presented on paper only in its externals, completely excluding his personal opinion of the matter, while above all observing every prescribed formality. The work was new and Ivan Ilych was one of the first men to apply the new Code of 1864.[1]

On taking up the post of examining magistrate in a new town, he made new acquaintances and connexions, placed himself on a new footing, and assumed a somewhat different tone. He took up an attitude of rather dignified aloofness towards the provincial authorities, but picked out the best circle of legal gentlemen and wealthy gentry living in the town and assumed a tone of slight dissatisfaction with the government, of moderate liberalism, and of enlightened citizenship. At the same time, without at all altering the elegance of his toilet, he ceased shaving his chin and allowed his beard to grow as it pleased.

Ivan Ilych settled down very pleasantly in this new town. The society there, which inclined towards opposition to the Governor, was friendly, his salary was larger, and he began to play *vint* [a form of bridge], which he found added not a little to the pleasure of life, for he had a capacity for cards, played good-humouredly, and calculated rapidly and astutely, so that he usually won.

After living there for two years he met his future wife, Praskovya Fedorovna Míkhel, who was the most attractive, clever, and brilliant girl of the set in which he moved, and among other amusements and relaxations from his labours as examining magistrate, Ivan Ilych established light and playful relations with her.

While he had been an official on special service he had been accustomed to dance, but now as an examining magistrate it was exceptional for him to do so. If he danced now, he did it as if to show that though he served under the reformed order of things, and had reached the fifth

[1] The emancipation of the serfs in 1861 was followed by a thorough all-round reform of judicial proceedings.

official rank, yet when it came to dancing he could do it better than most people. So at the end of an evening he sometimes danced with Praskovya Fedorovna, and it was chiefly during these dances that he captivated her. She fell in love with him. Ivan Ilych had at first no definite intention of marrying, but when the girl fell in love with him he said to himself: "Really, why shouldn't I marry?"

Praskovya Fedorovna came of a good family, was not bad looking, and had some little property. Ivan Ilych might have aspired to a more brilliant match, but even this was good. He had his salary, and she, he hoped, would have an equal income. She was well connected, and was a sweet, pretty, and thoroughly correct young woman. To say that Ivan Ilych married because he fell in love with Praskovya Fedorovna and found that she sympathized with his views of life would be as incorrect as to say that he married because his social circle approved of the match. He was swayed by both these considerations: the marriage gave him personal satisfaction, and at the same time it was considered the right thing by the most highly placed of his associates.

So Ivan Ilych got married.

The preparations for marriage and the beginning of married life, with its conjugal caresses, the new furniture, new crockery, and new linen, were very pleasant until his wife became pregnant—so that Ivan Ilych had begun to think that marriage would not impair the easy, agreeable, gay and always decorous character of his life, approved of by society and regarded by himself as natural, but would even improve it. But from the first months of his wife's pregnancy, something new, unpleasant, depressing, and unseemly, and from which there was no way of escape, unexpectedly showed itself.

His wife, without any reason—*de gaieté de cœur*[1] as Ivan Ilych expressed it to himself—began to disturb the pleasure and propriety of their life. She began to be jealous without any cause, expected him to devote his whole attention to her, found fault with everything, and made coarse and ill-mannered scenes.

At first Ivan Ilych hoped to escape from the unpleasantness of this state of affairs by the same easy and decorous relation to life that had served him heretofore: he tried to ignore his wife's disagreeable moods, continued to live in his usual easy and pleasant way, invited friends to his house for a game of cards, and also tried going out to his club or spending his evenings with friends. But one day his wife began upbraiding him so vigorously, using such coarse words, and continued to abuse him every time he did not fulfil her demands, so resolutely and with such evident

[1] [Spontaneously.]

determination not to give way till he submitted—that is, till he stayed at home and was bored just as she was—that he became alarmed. He now realized that matrimony—at any rate with Praskovya Fedorovna—was not always conducive to the pleasures and amenities of life, but on the contrary often infringed both comfort and propriety, and that he must therefore entrench himself against such infringement. And Ivan Ilych began to seek for means of doing so. His official duties were the one thing that imposed upon Praskovya Fedorovna, and by means of his official work and the duties attached to it he began struggling with his wife to secure his own independence.

With the birth of their child, the attempts to feed it and the various failures in doing so, and with the real and imaginary illnesses of mother and child, in which Ivan Ilych's sympathy was demanded but about which he understood nothing, the need of securing for himself an existence outside his family life became still more imperative.

As his wife grew more irritable and exacting and Ivan Ilych transferred the centre of gravity of his life more and more to his official work, so did he grow to like his work better and became more ambitious than before.

Very soon, within a year of his wedding, Ivan Ilych had realized that marriage, though it may add some comforts to life, is in fact a very intricate and difficult affair towards which in order to perform one's duty, that is, to lead a decorous life approved of by society, one must adopt a definite attitude just as towards one's official duties.

And Ivan Ilych evolved such an attitude towards married life. He only required of it those conveniences—dinner at home, housewife, and bed—which it could give him, and above all that propriety of external forms required by public opinion. For the rest he looked for light-hearted pleasure and propriety, and was very thankful when he found them, but if he met with antagonism and querulousness he at once retired into his separate fenced-off world of official duties, where he found satisfaction.

Ivan Ilych was esteemed a good official, and after three years was made Assistant Public Prosecutor. His new duties, their importance, the possibility of indicting and imprisoning anyone he chose, the publicity his speeches received, and the success he had in all these things, made his work still more attractive.

More children came. His wife became more and more querulous and ill-tempered, but the attitude Ivan Ilych had adopted towards his home life rendered him almost impervious to her grumbling.

After seven years' service in that town he was transferred to another province as Public Prosecutor. They moved, but were short of money and his wife did not like the place they moved to. Though the salary was higher the cost of living was greater, besides which two of their children died and family life became still more unpleasant for him.

Praskovya Fedorovna blamed her husband for every inconvenience they encountered in their new home. Most of the conversations between husband and wife, especially as to the children's education, led to topics which recalled former disputes, and those disputes were apt to flare up again at any moment. There remained only those rare periods of amorousness which still came to them at times but did not last long. These were islets at which they anchored for a while and then again set out upon that ocean of veiled hostility which showed itself in their aloofness from one another. This aloofness might have grieved Ivan Ilych had he considered that it ought not to exist, but he now regarded the position as normal, and even made it the goal at which he aimed in family life. His aim was to free himself more and more from those unpleasantnesses and to give them a semblance of harmlessness and propriety. He attained this by spending less and less time with his family, and when obliged to be at home he tried to safeguard his position by the presence of outsiders. The chief thing however was that he had his official duties. The whole interest of his life now centred in the official world and that interest absorbed him. The consciousness of his power, being able to ruin anybody he wished to ruin, the importance, even the external dignity of his entry into court, or meetings with his subordinates, his success with superiors and inferiors, and above all his masterly handling of cases, of which he was conscious—all this gave him pleasure and filled his life, together with chats with his colleagues, dinners, and bridge. So that on the whole Ivan Ilych's life continued to flow as he considered it should do—pleasantly and properly.

So things continued for another seven years. His eldest daughter was already sixteen, another child had died, and only one son was left, a schoolboy and a subject of dissension. Ivan Ilych wanted to put him in the School of Law, but to spite him Praskovya Fedorovna entered him at the High School. The daughter had been educated at home and had turned out well: the boy did not learn badly either.

III

So Ivan Ilych lived for seventeen years after his marriage. He was already a Public Prosecutor of long standing, and had declined several proposed transfers while awaiting a more desirable post, when an unanticipated and unpleasant occurrence quite upset the peaceful course of his life. He was expecting to be offered the post of presiding judge in a University town, but Happe somehow came to the front and obtained the appointment instead. Ivan Ilych became irritable, reproached Happe, and quarrelled both with him and with his immediate superiors—who became colder to him and again passed him over when other appointments were made.

This was in 1880, the hardest year of Ivan Ilych's life. It was then that it became evident on the one hand that his salary was insufficient for them to live on, and on the other that he had been forgotten, and not only this, but that what was for him the greatest and most cruel injustice appeared to others a quite ordinary occurrence. Even his father did not consider it his duty to help him. Ivan Ilych felt himself abandoned by everyone, and that they regarded his position with a salary of 3,500 rubles [about £350] as quite normal and even fortunate. He alone knew that with the consciousness of the injustices done him, with his wife's incessant nagging, and with the debts he had contracted by living beyond his means, his position was far from normal.

In order to save money that summer he obtained leave of absence and went with his wife to live in the country at her brother's place.

In the country, without his work, he experienced *ennui* for the first time in his life, and not only *ennui* but intolerable depression, and he decided that it was impossible to go on living like that, and that it was necessary to take energetic measures.

Having passed a sleepless night pacing up and down the veranda, he decided to go to Petersburg and bestir himself, in order to punish those who had failed to appreciate him and to get transferred to another ministry.

Next day, despite many protests from his wife and her brother, he started for Petersburg with the sole object of obtaining a post with a salary of five thousand rubles a year. He was no longer bent on any particular department, or tendency, or kind of activity. All he now wanted was an appointment to another post with a salary of five thousand rubles, either in the administration, in the banks, with the railways, in one of the Empress Márya's Institutions, or even in the customs—but it had to carry with it a salary of five thousand rubles and be in a ministry other than that in which they had failed to appreciate him.

And this quest of Ivan Ilych's was crowned with remarkable and unexpected success. At Kursk an acquaintance of his, F. I. Ilyín, got into the first-class carriage, sat down beside Ivan Ilych, and told him of a telegram just received by the Governor of Kursk announcing that a change was about to take place in the ministry: Peter Ivánovich was to be superseded by Iván Semënovich.

The proposed change, apart from its significance for Russia, had a special significance for Ivan Ilych, because by bringing forward a new man, Peter Petróvich, and consequently his friend Zachár Ivánovich, it was highly favourable for Ivan Ilych, since Zachar Ivanovich was a friend and colleague of his.

In Moscow this news was confirmed, and on reaching Petersburg Ivan Ilych found Zachar Ivanovich and received a definite promise of an appointment in his former department of Justice.

A week later he telegraphed to his wife: "Zachar in Miller's place. I shall receive appointment on presentation of report."

Thanks to this change of personnel, Ivan Ilych had unexpectedly obtained an appointment in his former ministry which placed him two stages above his former colleagues besides giving him five thousand rubles salary and three thousand five hundred rubles for expenses connected with his removal. All his ill humour towards his former enemies and the whole department vanished, and Ivan Ilych was completely happy.

He returned to the country more cheerful and contented than he had been for a long time. Praskovya Fedorovna also cheered up and a truce was arranged between them. Ivan Ilych told of how he had been fêted by everybody in Petersburg, how all those who had been his enemies were put to shame and now fawned on him, how envious they were of his appointment, and how much everybody in Petersburg had liked him.

Praskovya Fedorovna listened to all this and appeared to believe it. She did not contradict anything, but only made plans for their life in the town to which they were going. Ivan Ilych saw with delight that these plans were his plans, that he and his wife agreed, and that, after a stumble, his life was regaining its due and natural character of pleasant lightheartedness and decorum.

Ivan Ilych had come back for a short time only, for he had to take up his new duties on the 10th of September. Moreover, he needed time to settle into the new place, to move all his belongings from the province, and to buy and order many additional things: in a word, to make such arrangements as he had resolved on, which were almost exactly what Praskovya Fedorovna too had decided on.

Now that everything had happened so fortunately, and that he and his wife were at one in their aims and moreover saw so little of one another, they got on together better than they had done since the first years of marriage. Ivan Ilych had thought of taking his family away with him at once, but the insistence of his wife's brother and her sister-in-law, who had suddenly become particularly amiable and friendly to him and his family, induced him to depart alone.

So he departed, and the cheerful state of mind induced by his success and by the harmony between his wife and himself, the one intensifying the other, did not leave him. He found a delightful house, just the thing both he and his wife had dreamt of. Spacious, lofty reception rooms in the old style, a convenient and dignified study, rooms for his wife and daughter, a study for his son—it might have been specially built for them. Ivan Ilych himself superintended the arrangements, chose the wall-papers, supplemented the furniture (preferably with antiques which he considered particularly *comme il faut*), and supervised the upholstering. Everything progressed and progressed and approached the ideal he had set himself: even when things were only half completed they exceeded his expectations. He saw what a refined and elegant character, free from vulgarity, it would all have when it was ready. On falling asleep he pictured to himself how the reception-room would look. Looking at the yet unfinished drawing-room he could see the fireplace, the screen, the what-not, the little chairs dotted here and there, the dishes and plates on the walls, and the bronzes, as they would be when everything was in place. He was pleased by the thought of how his wife and daughter, who shared his taste in this matter, would be impressed by it. They were certainly not expecting as much. He had been particularly successful in finding, and buying cheaply, antiques which gave a particularly aristocratic character to the whole place. But in his letters he intentionally understated everything in order to be able to surprise them. All this so absorbed him that his new duties—though he liked his official work—interested him less than he had expected. Sometimes he even had moments of absent-mindedness during the Court Sessions, and would consider whether he should have straight or curved cornices for his curtains. He was so interested in it all that he often did things himself, rearranging the furniture, or rehanging the curtains. Once when mounting a step-ladder to show the upholsterer, who did not understand, how he wanted the hangings draped, he made a false step and slipped, but being a strong and agile man he clung on and only knocked his side against the knob of the window frame. The bruised place was painful but the pain soon passed, and he felt particularly bright and well just then. He wrote: "I feel fifteen years younger." He thought he would have everything ready by September, but it dragged on till mid-October. But the result was charming not only in his eyes but to everyone who saw it.

In reality it was just what is usually seen in the houses of people of moderate means who want to appear rich, and therefore succeed only in resembling others like themselves: there were damasks, dark wood, plants, rugs, and dull and polished bronzes—all the things people of a certain class have in order to resemble other people of that class. His house was so like the others that it would never have been noticed, but to him it all seemed to be quite exceptional. He was very happy when he met his family at the station and brought them to the newly furnished house all lit up, where a footman in a white tie opened the door into the hall decorated with plants, and when they went on into the drawing-room and the study uttering exclamations of delight. He conducted them everywhere, drank in their praises eagerly, and beamed with pleasure. At tea that evening, when Praskovya Fedorovna among other things asked him about his fall, he laughed, and showed them how he had gone flying and had frightened the upholsterer.

"It's a good thing I'm a bit of an athlete. Another man might have been killed, but I merely knocked myself, just here; it hurts when it's touched, but it's passing off already—it's only a bruise."

So they began living in their new home—in which, as always happens, when they got thoroughly settled in they found they were just one room short—and with the increased income, which as always was just a little (some five hundred rubles) too little, but it was all very nice.

Things went particularly well at first, before everything was finally arranged and while something had still to be done: this thing bought, that thing ordered, another thing moved, and something else adjusted. Though there were some disputes between husband and wife, they were both so well satisfied and had so much to do that it all passed off without any serious quarrels. When nothing was left to arrange it became rather dull and something seemed to be lacking, but they were then making acquaintances, forming habits, and life was growing fuller.

Ivan Ilych spent his mornings at the law court and came home to dinner, and at first he was generally in a good humour, though he occasionally became irritable just on account of his house. (Every spot on the tablecloth or the upholstery, and every broken window-blind string, irritated him. He had devoted so much trouble to arranging it all that every disturbance of it distressed him.) But on the whole his life ran its course as he believed life should do: easily, pleasantly, and decorously.

He got up at nine, drank his coffee, read the paper, and then put on his undress uniform and went to the law courts. There the harness in which he worked had already been stretched to fit him and he donned it without a hitch: petitioners, inquiries at the chancery, the chancery itself, and the sittings public and administrative. In all this the thing was to exclude everything fresh and vital, which always disturbs the regular course of official business, and to admit only official relations with people, and then only on official grounds. A man would come, for instance, wanting some information. Ivan Ilych, as one in whose sphere the matter did not lie, would have nothing to do with him: but if the man had some business with him in his official capacity, something that could be expressed on officially stamped paper, he would do everything, positively everything he could within the limits of such relations, and in doing so would maintain the semblance of friendly human relations, that is, would observe the courtesies of life. As soon as the official relations ended, so did everything else. Ivan Ilych possessed this capacity to separate his real life from the official side of affairs and not mix the two, in the highest degree, and by long practice and natural aptitude had brought it to such a pitch that sometimes, in the manner of a virtuoso, he would even allow himself to let the human and official relations mingle. He let himself do this just because he felt that he could at any time he chose resume the strictly official attitude again and drop the human relation. And he did it all easily, pleasantly, correctly, and even artistically. In the intervals between the sessions he smoked, drank tea, chatted a little about politics, a little about general topics, a little about cards, but most of all about official appointments. Tired, but with the feelings of a virtuoso—one of the first violins who has played his part in an orchestra with precision—he would return home to find that his wife and daughter had been out paying calls, or had a visitor, and that his son had been to school, had done his homework with his tutor, and was duly learning what is taught at High Schools. Everything was as it should be. After dinner, if they had no visitors, Ivan Ilych sometimes read a book that was being much discussed at the time, and in the evening settled down to work, that is, read official papers, compared the depositions of witnesses, and noted paragraphs of the Code applying to them. This was neither dull nor amusing. It was dull when he might have been playing bridge, but if no bridge was available it was at any rate better than doing nothing or sitting with his wife. Ivan Ilych's chief pleasure was giving little dinners to which he invited men and women of good social position, and just as his drawing-room resembled all other drawing-rooms so did his enjoyable little parties resemble all other such parties.

Once they even gave a dance. Ivan Ilych enjoyed it and everything went off well, except that it led to a violent quarrel with his wife about the cakes and sweets. Praskovya Fedorovna had made her own plans, but Ivan Ilych insisted on getting everything from an expensive confectioner and ordered too many cakes, and the quarrel occurred because some of those cakes were left over and the confectioner's bill came to forty-five rubles. It was a great and disagreeable quarrel. Praskovya Fedorovna called him "a fool and an imbecile," and he clutched at his head and made angry allusions to divorce.

But the dance itself had been enjoyable. The best people were there, and Ivan Ilych had danced with Princess Trúfonova, a sister of the distinguished founder of the Society "Bear My Burden."

The pleasures connected with his work were pleasures of ambition; his social pleasures were those of vanity; but Ivan Ilych's greatest pleasure was playing bridge. He acknowledged that whatever disagreeable incident happened in his life, the pleasure that beamed like a ray of light above everything else was to sit down to bridge with good players, not noisy partners, and of course to four-handed bridge (with five players it was annoying to have to stand out, though one pretended not to mind), to play a clever and serious game (when the cards allowed it) and then to have supper and drink a glass of wine. After a game of bridge, especially if he had won a little (to win a large sum was unpleasant), Ivan Ilych went to bed in specially good humour.

So they lived. They formed a circle of acquaintances among the best people and were visited by people of importance and by young folk. In their views as to their acquaintances, husband, wife and daughter were entirely agreed, and tacitly and unanimously kept at arm's length and shook off the various shabby friends and relations who, with much show of affection, gushed into the drawing-room with its Japanese plates on the walls. Soon these shabby friends ceased to obtrude themselves and only the best people remained in the Golovins' set.

Young men made up to Lisa, and Petríschhev, an examining magistrate and Dmítri Ivánovich Petrishchev's son and sole heir, began to be so attentive to her that Ivan Ilych had already spoken to Praskovya Fedorovna about it, and considered whether they should not arrange a party for them, or get up some private theatricals.

So they lived, and all went well, without change, and life flowed pleasantly.

IV

They were all in good health. It could not be called ill health if Ivan Ilych sometimes said that he had a queer taste in his mouth and felt some discomfort in his left side.

But this discomfort increased and, though not exactly painful, grew into a sense of pressure in his side accompanied by ill humour. And his irritability became worse and worse and began to mar the agreeable, easy, and correct life that had established itself in the Golovin family. Quarrels between husband and wife became more and more frequent, and soon the ease and amenity disappeared and even the decorum was barely maintained. Scenes again became frequent, and very few of those islets remained on which husband and wife could meet without an explosion. Praskovya Fedorovna now had good reason to say that her husband's temper was trying. With characteristic exaggeration she said he had always had a dreadful temper, and that it had needed all her good nature to put up with it for twenty years. It was true that now the quarrels were started by him. His bursts of temper always came just before dinner, often just as he began to eat his soup. Sometimes he noticed that a plate or dish was chipped, or the food was not right, or his son put his elbow on the table, or his daughter's hair was not done as he liked it, and for all this he blamed Praskovya Fedorovna. At first she retorted and said disagreeable things to him, but once or twice he fell into such a rage at the beginning of dinner that she realized it was due to some physical derangement brought on by taking food, and so she restrained herself and did not answer, but only hurried to get the dinner over. She regarded this self-restraint as highly praiseworthy. Having come to the conclusion that her husband had a dreadful temper and made her life miserable, she began to feel sorry for herself, and the more she pitied herself the more she hated her husband. She began to wish he would die; yet she did not want him to die because then his salary would cease. And this irritated her against him still more. She considered herself dreadfully unhappy just because not even his death could save her, and though she concealed her exasperation, that hidden exasperation of hers increased his irritation also.

After one scene in which Ivan Ilych had been particularly unfair and after which he had said in explanation that he certainly was irritable but that it was due to his not being well, she said that if he was ill it should be attended to, and insisted on his going to see a celebrated doctor.

He went. Everything took place as he had expected and as it always does. There was the usual waiting and the important air assumed by the doctor, with which he was so familiar (resembling that which he himself assumed in court), and the sounding and listening, and the questions which called for answers that were foregone conclusions and were evidently unnecessary, and the look of importance which implied that "if only you put yourself in our hands we will arrange everything—we know indubitably how it has to be done, always in the same way for everybody alike." It was all just as it was in the law courts. The doctor put on just the same air towards him as he himself put on towards an accused person.

The doctor said that so-and-so indicated that there was so-and-so inside the patient, but if the investigation of so-and-so did not confirm this, then he must assume that and that. If he assumed that and that, then . . . and so on. To Ivan Ilych only one question was important: was his case serious or not? But the doctor ignored that inappropriate question. From his point of view it was not the one under consideration, the real question was to decide between a floating kidney, chronic catarrh, or appendicitis. It was not a question of Ivan Ilych's life or death, but one between a floating kidney and appendicitis. And that question the doctor solved brilliantly, as it seemed to Ivan Ilych, in favour of the appendix, with the reservation that should an examination of the urine give fresh indications the matter would be reconsidered. All this was just what Ivan Ilych had himself brilliantly accomplished a thousand times in dealing with men on trial. The doctor summed up just as brilliantly, looking over his spectacles triumphantly and even gaily at the accused. From the doctor's summing up Ivan Ilych concluded that things were bad, but that for the doctor, and perhaps for everybody else, it was a matter of indifference, though for him it was bad. And this conclusion struck him painfully, arousing in him a great feeling of pity for himself and of bitterness towards the doctor's indifference to a matter of such importance.

He said nothing of this, but rose, placed the doctor's fee on the table, and remarked with a sigh: "We sick people probably often put inappropriate questions. But tell me, in general, is this complaint dangerous, or not? . . ."

The doctor looked at him sternly over his spectacles with one eye, as if to say: "Prisoner, if you will not keep to the questions put to you, I shall be obliged to have you removed from the court."

"I have already told you what I consider necessary and proper. The analysis may show something more." And the doctor bowed.

Ivan Ilych went out slowly, seated himself disconsolately in his sledge, and drove home. All the way home he was going over what the doctor had said, trying to translate those complicated, obscure, scientific phrases into plain language and find in them an answer to the question: "Is my condition bad? Is it very bad? Or is there as yet nothing much wrong?" And it seemed to him that the meaning of what the doctor had said was that it was very bad. Everything in the streets seemed depressing. The cabmen, the houses, the passers-by, and the shops, were dismal. His ache, this dull gnawing ache that never ceased for a moment, seemed to have acquired a new and more serious significance from the doctor's dubious remarks. Ivan Ilych now watched it with a new and oppressive feeling.

He reached home and began to tell his wife about it. She listened, but in the middle of his account his daughter came in with her hat on, ready to go out with her mother. She sat down reluctantly to listen to this tedious story, but could not stand it long, and her mother too did not hear him to the end.

"Well, I am very glad," she said. "Mind now to take your medicine regularly. Give me the prescription and I'll send Gerasim to the chemist's." And she went to get ready to go out.

While she was in the room Ivan Ilych had hardly taken time to breathe, but he sighed deeply when she left it.

"Well," he thought, "perhaps it isn't so bad after all."

He began taking his medicine and following the doctor's directions, which had been altered after the examination of the urine. But then it happened that there was a contradiction between the indications drawn from the examination of the urine and the symptoms that showed themselves. It turned out that what was happening differed from what the doctor had told him, and that he had either forgotten, or blundered, or hidden something from him. He could not, however, be blamed for that, and Ivan Ilych still obeyed his orders implicitly and at first derived some comfort from doing so.

From the time of his visit to the doctor, Ivan Ilych's chief occupation was the exact fulfilment of the doctor's instructions regarding hygiene and the taking of medicine, and the observation of his pain and his excretions. His chief interests came to be people's ailments and people's health. When sickness, deaths, or recoveries were mentioned in his presence, especially when the illness resembled his own, he listened with agitation which he tried to hide, asked questions, and applied what he heard to his own case.

The pain did not grow less, but Ivan Ilych made efforts to force himself to think that he was better. And he could do this so long as nothing agitated him. But as soon as he had any unpleasantness with his wife, any lack of success in his official work, or held bad cards at bridge, he was at once acutely sensible of his disease. He had formerly borne such mischances, hoping soon to adjust what was wrong, to master it and attain success, or make a grand slam. But now every mischance upset him and plunged him into despair. He would say to himself: "There now, just as I was beginning to get better and the medicine had begun to take effect, comes this accursed misfortune, or unpleasantness . . ." And he was furious with the mishap, or with the people who were causing the unpleasantness and killing him, for he felt that this fury was killing him but could not restrain it. One would have thought that it should have been clear to him that this exasperation with circumstances and people aggravated his illness, and that he ought therefore to ignore unpleasant occurrences. But he drew the very opposite conclusion: he said that he needed peace, and he watched for everything that might disturb it and became irritable at the slightest infringement of it. His condition was rendered worse by the fact that he read medical books and consulted doctors. The progress of his disease was so gradual that he could deceive himself when comparing one day with another—the difference was so slight. But when he consulted the doctors it seemed to him that he was getting worse, and even very rapidly. Yet despite this he was continually consulting them.

That month he went to see another celebrity, who told him almost the same as the first had done but put his questions rather differently, and the interview with this celebrity only increased Ivan Ilych's doubts and fears. A friend of a friend of his, a very good doctor, diagnosed his illness again quite differently from the others, and though he predicted recovery, his questions and suppositions bewildered Ivan Ilych still more and increased his doubts. A homoeopathist diagnosed the disease in yet another way, and prescribed medicine which Ivan Ilych took secretly for a week. But after a week, not feeling any improvement and having lost confidence both in the former doctor's treatment and in this one's, he became still more despondent. One day a lady acquaintance mentioned a cure effected by a wonder-working icon. Ivan Ilych caught himself listening attentively and beginning to believe that it had occurred. This incident alarmed him. "Has my mind really weakened to such an extent?" he asked himself. "Nonsense! It's all rubbish. I mustn't give way to nervous fears but having chosen a doctor must keep strictly to his treatment. That is what I will do. Now it's all settled. I won't think about it, but will follow the treatment seriously till summer, and then we shall see. From now there must be no more of this wavering!" This was easy to say but impossible to carry out. The pain in his side oppressed him and seemed to grow worse and more incessant, while the taste in his mouth grew stranger and stranger. It seemed to him that his breath had a disgusting smell, and he was conscious of a loss of appetite and strength. There was no deceiving himself: something terrible, new, and more important than anything before in his life, was taking place within him of which he alone was aware. Those about him did not understand or would not understand it, but thought everything in the world was going on as usual. That tormented Ivan Ilych more than anything. He saw that his household, especially his wife and daughter who were in a perfect whirl of visiting, did not understand anything of it and were annoyed that he was so depressed and so exacting, as if he were to blame for it. Though they tried to disguise it he saw that he was an obstacle in their path, and that his wife had adopted a definite line in regard to his illness and kept to it regardless of anything he said or did. Her attitude was this: "You know," she would say to her friends, "Ivan Ilych can't do as other people do, and keep to the treatment prescribed for him. One day he'll take his drops and keep strictly to his diet and go to bed in good time, but the next day unless I watch him he'll suddenly forget his medicine, eat sturgeon—which is forbidden—and sit up playing cards till one o'clock in the morning."

"Oh, come, when was that?" Ivan Ilych would ask in vexation. "Only once at Peter Ivanovich's."

"And yesterday with Shebek."

"Well, even if I hadn't stayed up, this pain would have kept me awake."

"Be that as it may you'll never get well like that, but will always make us wretched."

Praskovya Fedorovna's attitude to Ivan Ilych's illness, as she expressed it both to others and to him, was that it was his own fault and was another of the annoyances he caused her. Ivan Ilych felt that this opinion escaped her involuntarily—but that did not make it easier for him.

At the law courts too, Ivan Ilych noticed, or thought he noticed, a strange attitude towards himself. It sometimes seemed to him that people were watching him inquisitively as a man whose place might soon be vacant. Then again, his friends would suddenly begin to chaff him in a friendly way about his low spirits, as if the awful, horrible, and unheard-of thing that was going on within him, incessantly gnawing at him and irresistibly drawing him away, was a very agreeable subject for jests. Schwartz in particular irritated him by his jocularity, vivacity, and *savoir-faire*,[1] which reminded him of what he himself had been ten years ago.

Friends came to make up a set and they sat down to cards. They dealt, bending the new cards to soften them, and he sorted the diamonds in his hand and found he had seven. His partner said "No trumps" and supported him with two diamonds. What more could be wished for? It ought to be jolly and lively. They would make a grand slam. But suddenly Ivan Ilych was conscious of that gnawing pain, that taste in his mouth, and it seemed ridiculous that in such circumstances he should be pleased to make a grand slam.

He looked at his partner Mikháil Mikháylovich, who rapped the table with his strong hand and instead of snatching up the tricks pushed the cards courteously and indulgently towards Ivan Ilych that he might have the pleasure of gathering them up without the trouble of stretching out his hand for them. "Does he think I am too weak to stretch out my arm?" thought Ivan Ilych, and forgetting what he was doing he over-trumped his partner, missing the grand slam by three tricks. And what was most awful of all was that he saw how upset Mikhail Mikhaylovich was about it

[1] [Social adroitness.]

but did not himself care. And it was dreadful to realize why he did not care.

They all saw that he was suffering, and said: "We can stop if you are tired. Take a rest." Lie down? No, he was not at all tired, and he finished the rubber. All were gloomy and silent. Ivan Ilych felt that he had diffused this gloom over them and could not dispel it. They had supper and went away, and Ivan Ilych was left alone with the consciousness that his life was poisoned and was poisoning the lives of others, and that this poison did not weaken but penetrated more and more deeply into his whole being.

With this consciousness, and with physical pain besides the terror, he must go to bed, often to lie awake the greater part of the night. Next morning he had to get up again, dress, go to the law courts, speak, and write; or if he did not go out, spend at home those twenty-four hours a day each of which was a torture. And he had to live thus all alone on the brink of an abyss, with no one who understood or pitied him.

V

So one month passed and then another. Just before the New Year his brother-in-law came to town and stayed at their house. Ivan Ilych was at the law courts and Praskovya Fedorovna had gone shopping. When Ivan Ilych came home and entered his study he found his brother-in-law there—a healthy, florid man—unpacking his portmanteau himself. He raised his head on hearing Ivan Ilych's footsteps and looked up at him for a moment without a word. That stare told Ivan Ilych everything. His brother-in-law opened his mouth to utter an exclamation of surprise but checked himself, and that action confirmed it all.

"I have changed, eh?"

"Yes, there is a change."

And after that, try as he would to get his brother-in-law to return to the subject of his looks, the latter would say nothing about it. Praskovya Fedorovna came home and her brother went out to her. Ivan Ilych locked the door and began to examine himself in the glass, first full face, then in profile. He took up a portrait of himself taken with his wife, and compared it with what he saw in the glass. The change in him was immense. Then he bared his arms to the elbow, looked at them, drew the sleeves down again, sat down on an ottoman, and grew blacker than night.

"No, no, this won't do!" he said to himself, and jumped up, went to the table, took up some law papers and began to read them, but could not continue. He unlocked the door and went into the reception-room. The door leading to the drawing-room was shut. He approached it on tiptoe and listened.

"No, you are exaggerating!" Praskovya Fedorovna was saying.

"Exaggerating! Don't you see it? Why, he's a dead man! Look at his eyes—there's no light in them. But what is it that is wrong with him?"

"No one knows. Nikoláevich [that was another doctor] said something, but I don't know what. And Leshchetítsky [this was the celebrated specialist] said quite the contrary . . ."

Ivan Ilych walked away, went to his own room, lay down, and began musing: "The kidney, a floating kidney." He recalled all the doctors had told him of how it detached itself and swayed about. And by an effort of imagination he tried to catch that kidney and arrest it and support it. So little was needed for this, it seemed to him. "No, I'll go to see Peter Ivanovich again." [That was the friend whose friend was a doctor.] He rang, ordered the carriage, and got ready to go.

"Where are you going, Jean?" asked his wife, with a specially sad and exceptionally kind look.

This exceptionally kind look irritated him. He looked morosely at her.

"I must go to see Peter Ivanovich."

He went to see Peter Ivanovich, and together they went to see his friend, the doctor. He was in, and Ivan Ilych had a long talk with him.

Reviewing the anatomical and physiological details of what in the doctor's opinion was going on inside him, he understood it all.

There was something, a small thing, in the vermiform appendix. It might all come right. Only stimulate the energy of one organ and check the activity of another, then absorption would take place and everything would come right. He got home rather late for dinner, ate his dinner, and conversed cheerfully, but could not for a long time bring himself to go back to work in his room. At last, however, he went to his study and did what was necessary, but the consciousness that he had put something aside—an important, intimate matter which he would revert to when his work was done—never left him. When he had finished his work he remembered that this intimate matter was the thought of his vermiform appendix. But he did not give himself up to it, and went to the drawing-room for tea. There were callers there, including the examining magistrate who was a desirable match for his daughter, and they were conversing, playing the piano, and singing. Ivan Ilych, as Praskovya Fedorovna remarked, spent that evening more cheerfully than usual, but he never for a moment forgot that he had postponed the important matter of the appendix. At eleven o'clock he said good-night and went to his bedroom. Since his illness he had slept alone in a small room next to his study. He undressed and took up a novel by Zola, but instead of reading it he fell into thought, and in his imagination that desired improvement in the vermiform appendix occurred. There was the absorption and evacuation and the re-establishment of normal activity. "Yes, that's it!" he said to himself. "One need only assist nature, that's all." He remembered his medicine, rose, took it, and lay down on his back watching for the beneficent action of the medicine and for it to lessen the pain. "I need only take it regularly and avoid all injurious influences. I am already feeling better, much better." He began touching his side: it was not painful to the touch. "There, I really don't feel it. It's much better already." He put out the light and turned on his side . . . "The appendix is getting better, absorption is occurring." Suddenly he felt the old, familiar, dull, gnawing pain, stubborn and serious. There was the same familiar loathsome taste in his mouth. His heart sank and he felt dazed. "My God! My God!" he muttered. "Again, again! And it will never cease." And suddenly the matter presented itself in a quite different aspect. "Vermiform appendix! Kidney!" he said to himself. "It's not a question of appendix or kidney, but of life and . . . death. Yes, life was there and now it is going, going and I cannot stop it. Yes. Why deceive myself? Isn't it obvious to everyone but me that I'm dying, and that it's only a question of weeks, days . . . it may happen this moment. There was light and now there is darkness. I was here and now I'm going there! Where?" A chill came over him, his breathing ceased, and he felt only the throbbing of his heart.

"When I am not, what will there be? There will be nothing. Then where shall I be when I am no more? Can this be dying? No, I don't want to!" He jumped up and tried to light the candle, felt for it with trembling hands, dropped candle and candlestick on the floor, and fell back on his pillow.

"What's the use? It makes no difference," he said to himself, staring with wide-open eyes into the darkness. "Death. Yes, death. And none of them know or wish to know it, and they have no pity for me. Now they are playing." (He heard through the door the distant sound of a song and its accompaniment.) "It's all the same to them, but they will die too! Fools! I first, and they later, but it will be the same for them. And now they are merry . . . the beasts!"

Anger choked him and he was agonizingly, unbearably miserable. "It is impossible that all men have been doomed to suffer this awful horror!" He raised himself.

"Something must be wrong. I must calm myself—must think it all over from the beginning." And he again began thinking. "Yes, the beginning of my illness: I knocked my side, but I was still quite well that day and the next. It hurt a little, then rather more. I saw the doctors, then followed despondency and anguish, more doctors, and I drew nearer to the abyss. My strength grew less and I kept coming nearer and nearer, and now I have wasted away and there is no light in my eyes. I think of the appendix—but this is death! I think of mending the appendix, and all the while here is death! Can it really be death?" Again terror seized him and he gasped for breath. He leant down and began feeling for the matches, pressing with his elbow on the stand beside the bed. It was in his way and hurt him, he grew furious with it, pressed on it still harder, and upset it. Breathless and in despair he fell on his back, expecting death to come immediately.

Meanwhile the visitors were leaving. Praskovya Fedorovna was seeing them off. She heard something fall and came in.

"What has happened?"

"Nothing. I knocked it over accidentally."

She went out and returned with a candle. He lay there panting heavily, like a man who has run a thousand yards, and stared upwards at her with a fixed look.

"What is it, Jean?"

"No . . . o . . . thing. I upset it." ("Why speak of it? She won't understand," he thought.)

And in truth she did not understand. She picked up the stand, lit his candle, and hurried away to see another visitor off. When she came back he still lay on his back, looking upwards.

"What is it? Do you feel worse?"

"Yes."

She shook her head and sat down.

"Do you know, Jean, I think we must ask Leshchetitsky to come and see you here."

This meant calling in the famous specialist, regardless of expense. He smiled malignantly and said "No." She remained a little longer and then went up to him and kissed his forehead.

While she was kissing him he hated her from the bottom of his soul and with difficulty refrained from pushing her away.

"Good-night. Please God you'll sleep."

"Yes."

VI

Ivan Ilych saw that he was dying, and he was in continual despair.

In the depth of his heart he knew he was dying, but not only was he not accustomed to the thought, he simply did not and could not grasp it.

The syllogism he had learnt from Kiezewetter's Logic: "Caius is a man, men are mortal, therefore Caius is mortal," had always seemed to him correct as applied to Caius, but certainly not as applied to himself. That Caius—man in the abstract—was mortal, was perfectly correct, but he was not Caius, not an abstract man, but a creature quite, quite separate from all others. He had been little Ványa, with a mamma and a papa, with Mítya and Volódya, with the toys, a coachman and a nurse, afterwards with Kátenka and with all the joys, griefs, and delights of childhood, boyhood, and youth. What did Caius know of the smell of that striped leather ball Vanya had been so fond of? Had Caius kissed his mother's hand like that, and did the silk of her dress rustle so for Caius? Had he rioted like that at school when the pastry was bad? Had Caius been in love like that? Could Caius preside at a session as he did? "Caius really was mortal, and it was right for him to die; but for me, little Vanya, Ivan Ilych, with all my thoughts and emotions, it's altogether a different matter. It cannot be that I ought to die. That would be too terrible."

Such was his feeling.

"If I had to die like Caius I should have known it was so. An inner voice would have told me so, but there was nothing of the sort in me and I and all my friends felt that our case was quite different from that of Caius. And now here it is!" he said to himself. "It can't be. It's impossible! But here it is. How is this? How is one to understand it?"

He could not understand it, and tried to drive this false, incorrect, morbid thought away and to replace it by other proper and healthy thoughts. But that thought, and not the thought only but the reality itself, seemed to come and confront him.

And to replace that thought he called up a succession of others, hoping to find in them some support. He tried to get back into the former current of thoughts that had once screened the thought of death from him. But strange to say, all that had formerly shut off, hidden, and destroyed his consciousness of death, no longer had that effect. Ivan Ilych now spent most of his time in attempting to re-establish that old current. He would say to himself: "I will take up my duties again—after all I used to live by them." And banishing all doubts he would go to the law courts, enter into conversation with his colleagues, and sit carelessly as was his wont, scanning the crowd with a thoughtful look and leaning both his emaciated arms on the arms of his oak chair; bending over as usual to a colleague and drawing his papers nearer he would interchange whispers with him, and then suddenly raising his eyes and sitting erect would pronounce certain words and open the proceedings. But suddenly in the midst of those proceedings the pain in his side, regardless of the stage the proceedings had reached, would begin its own gnawing work. Ivan Ilych would turn his attention to it and try to drive the thought of it away, but without success. *It* would come and stand before him and look at him, and he would be petrified and the light would die out of his eyes, and he would again begin asking himself whether *It* alone was true. And his colleagues and subordinates would see with surprise and distress that he, the brilliant and subtle judge, was becoming confused and making mistakes. He would shake himself, try to pull himself together, manage somehow to bring the sitting to a close, and return home with the sorrowful consciousness that his judicial labours could not as formerly hide from him what he wanted them to hide, and could not deliver him from *It*. And what was worst of all was that *It* drew his attention to itself not in order to make him take some action but only that he should look at *It*, look it straight in the face: look at it and without doing anything, suffer inexpressibly.

And to save himself from this condition Ivan Ilych looked for consolations—new screens—and new screens were found and for a while seemed to save him, but then they immediately fell to pieces or rather became transparent, as if *It* penetrated them and nothing could veil *It*.

In these latter days he would go into the drawing-room he had arranged—that drawing-room where he had fallen and for the sake of which (how bitterly ridiculous it seemed) he had sacrificed his life—for he knew that his illness originated with that knock. He would enter and see that something had scratched the polished table. He would look for the cause of this and find that it was the bronze ornamentation of an album, that had got bent. He would take up the expensive album which he had lovingly arranged, and feel vexed with his daughter and her friends for their untidiness—for the album was torn here and there and some of the photographs turned upside down. He would put it carefully in order and bend the ornamentation back into position. Then it would occur to him to place all those things in another corner of the room, near the plants. He would call the footman, but his daughter or wife would come to help him. They would not agree, and his wife would contradict him, and he would dispute and grow angry. But that was all right, for then he did not think about *It*. *It* was invisible.

But then, when he was moving something himself, his wife would say: "Let the servants do it. You will hurt yourself again." And suddenly *It* would flash through the screen and he would see it. It was just a flash, and he hoped it would disappear, but he would involuntarily pay attention to his side. "It sits there as before, gnawing just the same!" And he could no longer forget *It*, but could distinctly see it looking at him from behind the flowers. "What is it all for?"

"It really is so! I lost my life over that curtain as I might have done when storming a fort. Is that possible? How terrible and how stupid. It can't be true! It can't, but it is."

He would go to his study, lie down, and again be alone with *It*: face to face with *It*. And nothing could be done with *It* except to look at it and shudder.

VII

How it happened it is impossible to say because it came about step by step, unnoticed, but in the third month of Ivan Ilych's illness, his wife, his daughter, his son, his acquaintances, the doctors, the servants, and above all he himself, were aware that the whole interest he had for other people was whether he would soon vacate his place, and at last release the living from the discomfort caused by his presence and be himself released from his sufferings.

He slept less and less. He was given opium and hypodermic injections of morphine, but this did not relieve him. The dull depression he experienced in a somnolent condition at first gave him a little relief, but only as something new, afterwards it became as distressing as the pain itself or even more so.

Special foods were prepared for him by the doctors' orders, but all those foods became increasingly distasteful and disgusting to him.

For his excretions also special arrangements had to be made, and this was a torment to him every time—a torment from the uncleanliness, the unseemliness, and the smell, and from knowing that another person had to take part in it.

But just through this most unpleasant matter, Ivan Ilych obtained comfort. Gerasim, the butler's young assistant, always came in to carry the things out. Gerasim was a clean, fresh peasant lad, grown stout on town food and always cheerful and bright. At first the sight of him, in his clean Russian peasant costume, engaged on that disgusting task embarrassed Ivan Ilych.

Once when he got up from the commode too weak to draw up his trousers, he dropped into a soft armchair and looked with horror at his bare, enfeebled thighs with the muscles so sharply marked on them.

Gerasim with a firm light tread, his heavy boots emitting a pleasant smell of tar and fresh winter air, came in wearing a clean Hessian apron, the sleeves of his print shirt tucked up over his strong bare young arms; and refraining from looking at his sick master out of consideration for his feelings, and restraining the joy of life that beamed from his face, he went up to the commode.

"Gerasim!" said Ivan Ilych in a weak voice.

Gerasim started, evidently afraid he might have committed some blunder, and with a rapid movement turned his fresh, kind, simple young face which just showed the first downy signs of a beard.

"Yes, sir?"

"That must be very unpleasant for you. You must forgive me. I am helpless."

"Oh, why, sir," and Gerasim's eyes beamed and he showed his glistening white teeth, "what's a little trouble? It's a case of illness with you, sir."

And his deft strong hands did their accustomed task, and he went out of the room stepping lightly. Five minutes later he as lightly returned.

Ivan Ilych was still sitting in the same position in the armchair.

"Gerasim," he said when the latter had replaced the freshly-washed utensil. "Please come here and help me." Gerasim went up to him. "Lift me up. It is hard for me to get up, and I have sent Dmitri away."

Gerasim went up to him, grasped his master with his strong arms deftly but gently, in the same way that he stepped—lifted him, supported him with one hand, and with the other drew up his trousers and would have set him down again, but Ivan Ilych asked to be led to the sofa. Gerasim, without an effort and without apparent pressure, led him, almost lifting him, to the sofa and placed him on it.

"Thank you. How easily and well you do it all!"

Gerasim smiled again and turned to leave the room. But Ivan Ilych felt his presence such a comfort that he did not want to let him go.

"One thing more, please move up that chair. No, the other one—under my feet. It is easier for me when my feet are raised."

Gerasim brought the chair, set it down gently in place, and raised Ivan Ilych's legs on to it. It seemed to Ivan Ilych that he felt better while Gerasim was holding up his legs.

"It's better when my legs are higher," he said. "Place that cushion under them."

Gerasim did so. He again lifted the legs and placed them, and again Ivan Ilych felt better while Gerasim held his legs. When he set them down Ivan Ilych fancied he felt worse.

"Gerasim," he said. "Are you busy now?"

"Not at all, sir," said Gerasim, who had learnt from the townsfolk how to speak to gentlefolk.

"What have you still to do?"

"What have I to do? I've done everything except chopping the logs for to-morrow."

"Then hold my legs up a bit higher, can you?"

"Of course I can. Why not?" And Gerasim raised his master's legs higher and Ivan Ilych thought that in that position he did not feel any pain at all.

"And how about the logs?"

"Don't trouble about that, sir. There's plenty of time."

Ivan Ilych told Gerasim to sit down and hold his legs, and began to talk to him. And strange to say it seemed to him that he felt better while Gerasim held his legs up.

After that Ivan Ilych would sometimes call Gerasim and get him to hold his legs on his shoulders, and he liked talking to him. Gerasim did it all easily, willingly, simply, and with a good nature that touched Ivan Ilych. Health, strength, and vitality in other people were offensive to him, but Gerasim's strength and vitality did not mortify but soothed him.

What tormented Ivan Ilych most was the deception, the lie, which for some reason they all accepted, that he was not dying but was simply ill, and that he only need keep quiet and undergo a treatment and then something very good would result. He however knew that do what they would nothing would come of it, only still more agonizing suffering and death. This deception tortured him—their not wishing to admit what they all knew and what he knew, but wanting to lie to him concerning his terrible condition, and wishing and forcing him to participate in that lie. Those lies—lies enacted over him on the eve of his death and destined to degrade this awful, solemn act to the level of their visitings, their curtains, their sturgeon for dinner—were a terrible agony for Ivan Ilych. And strangely enough, many times when they were going through their antics over him he had been within a hairbreadth of calling out to them: "Stop lying! You know and I know that I am dying. Then at least stop lying about it!" But he had never had the spirit to do it. The awful, terrible act of his dying was, he could see, reduced by those about him to the level of a casual, unpleasant, and almost indecorous incident (as if someone entered a drawing-room diffusing an unpleasant odour) and this was done by that very decorum which he had served all his life long. He saw that no one felt for him, because no one even wished to grasp his position. Only Gerasim recognized it and pitied him. And so Ivan Ilych felt at ease only with him. He felt comforted when Gerasim supported his legs (sometimes all night long) and refused to go to bed, saying: "Don't you worry, Ivan Ilych. I'll get sleep enough later on," or when he suddenly became familiar and exclaimed: "If you weren't sick it would be another matter, but as it is, why should I grudge a little trouble?" Gerasim alone did not lie; everything showed that he alone understood the facts of the case and did not consider it necessary to disguise them, but simply felt sorry for his emaciated and enfeebled master. Once when Ivan Ilych was sending him away he even said straight out: "We shall all of us die, so why should I grudge a little trouble?"—expressing the fact that he did not think his work burdensome, because he was doing it for a dying man and hoped someone would do the same for him when his time came.

Apart from this lying, or because of it, what most tormented Ivan Ilych was that no one pitied him as he wished to be pitied. At certain moments after prolonged suffering he wished most of all (though he would have been ashamed to confess it) for someone to pity him as a sick child is pitied. He longed to be petted and comforted. He knew he was an important functionary, that he had a beard turning grey, and that therefore what he longed for was impossible, but still he longed for it. And in Gerasim's attitude towards him there was something akin to what he wished for, and so that attitude comforted him. Ivan Ilych wanted to weep, wanted to be petted and cried over, and then his colleague Shebek would come, and instead of weeping and being petted, Ivan Ilych would assume a serious, severe, and profound air, and by force of habit would express his opinion on a decision of the Court of Cassation and would stubbornly insist on that view. This falsity around him and within him did more than anything else to poison his last days.

VIII

It was morning. He knew it was morning because Gerasim had gone, and Peter the footman had come and put out the candles, drawn back one of the curtains, and begun quietly to tidy up. Whether it was morning or evening, Friday or Sunday, made no difference, it was all just the same: the gnawing, unmitigated, agonizing pain, never ceasing for an instant, the consciousness of life inexorably waning but not yet extinguished, the approach of that ever dreaded and hateful Death which was the only reality, and always the same falsity. What were days, weeks, hours, in such a case?

"Will you have some tea, sir?"

"He wants things to be regular, and wishes the gentlefolk to drink tea in the morning," thought Ivan Ilych, and only said "No."

"Wouldn't you like to move onto the sofa, sir?"

"He wants to tidy up the room, and I'm in the way. I am uncleanliness and disorder," he thought, and said only:

"No, leave me alone."

The man went on bustling about. Ivan Ilych stretched out his hand. Peter came up, ready to help.

"What is it, sir?"

"My watch."

Peter took the watch which was close at hand and gave it to his master.

"Half-past eight. Are they up?"

"No sir, except Vladímir Ivánich" (the son) "who has gone to school. Praskovya Fedorovna ordered me to wake her if you asked for her. Shall I do so?"

"No, there's no need to." "Perhaps I'd better have some tea," he thought, and added aloud: "Yes, bring me some tea."

Peter went to the door, but Ivan Ilych dreaded being left alone. "How can I keep him here? Oh yes, my medicine." "Peter, give me my medicine." "Why not? Perhaps it may still do me some good." He took a spoonful and swallowed it. "No, it won't help. It's all tomfoolery, all deception," he decided as soon as he became aware of the familiar, sickly, hopeless taste. "No, I can't believe in it any longer. But the pain, why this pain? If it would only cease just for a moment!" And he moaned. Peter turned towards him. "It's all right. Go and fetch me some tea."

Peter went out. Left alone Ivan Ilych groaned not so much with pain, terrible though that was, as from mental anguish. Always and for ever the same, always these endless days and nights. If only it would come quicker! If only *what* would come quicker? Death, darkness? . . . No, no! Anything rather than death!

When Peter returned with the tea on a tray, Ivan Ilych stared at him for a time in perplexity, not realizing who and what he was. Peter was disconcerted by that look and his embarrassment brought Ivan Ilych to himself.

"Oh, tea! All right, put it down. Only help me to wash and put on a clean shirt."

And Ivan Ilych began to wash. With pauses for rest, he washed his hands and then his face, cleaned his teeth, brushed his hair, and looked in the glass. He was terrified by what he saw, especially by the limp way in which his hair clung to his pallid forehead.

While his shirt was being changed he knew that he would be still more frightened at the sight of his body, so he avoided looking at it. Finally he was ready. He drew on a dressing-gown, wrapped himself in a plaid, and sat down in the armchair to take his tea. For a moment he felt refreshed, but as soon as he began to drink the tea he was again aware of the same taste, and the pain also returned. He finished it with an effort, and then lay down stretching out his legs, and dismissed Peter.

Always the same. Now a spark of hope flashes up, then a sea of despair rages, and always pain; always pain, always despair, and always the same. When alone he had a dreadful and distressing desire to call someone, but he knew beforehand that with others present it would be still worse. "Another dose of morphine—to lose consciousness. I will tell him, the doctor, that he must think of something else. It's impossible, impossible, to go on like this."

An hour and another pass like that. But now there is a ring at the door bell. Perhaps it's the doctor? It is. He comes in fresh, hearty, plump, and cheerful, with that look on his face that seems to say: "There now, you're in a panic about something, but we'll arrange it all for you directly!" The doctor knows this expression is out of place here, but he has put it on once for all and can't take it off—like a man who has put on a frock-coat in the morning to pay a round of calls.

The doctor rubs his hands vigorously and reassuringly.

"Brr! How cold it is! There's such a sharp frost; just let me warm myself!" he says, as if it were only a matter of waiting till he was warm, and then he would put everything right.

"Well now, how are you?"

Ivan Ilych feels that the doctor would like to say: "Well, how are our affairs?" but that even he feels that this would not do, and says instead: "What sort of a night have you had?"

Ivan Ilych looks at him as much as to say: "Are you really never ashamed of lying?" But the doctor does not wish to understand this question, and Ivan Ilych says: "Just as terrible as ever. The pain never leaves me and never subsides. If only something . . ."

"Yes, you sick people are always like that. . . . There, now I think I am warm enough. Even Praskovya Fedorovna, who is so particular, could find no fault with my temperature. Well, now I can say good-morning," and the doctor presses his patient's hand.

Then, dropping his former playfulness, he begins with a most serious face to examine the patient, feeling his pulse and taking his temperature, and then begins the sounding and auscultation.

Ivan Ilych knows quite well and definitely that all this is nonsense and pure deception, but when the doctor, getting down on his knee, leans over him, putting his ear first higher then lower, and performs various gymnastic movements over him with a significant expression on his face,

Ivan Ilych submits to it all as he used to submit to the speeches of the lawyers, though he knew very well that they were all lying and why they were lying.

The doctor, kneeling on the sofa, is still sounding him when Praskovya Fedorovna's silk dress rustles at the door and she is heard scolding Peter for not having let her know of the doctor's arrival.

She comes in, kisses her husband, and at once proceeds to prove that she has been up a long time already, and only owing to a misunderstanding failed to be there when the doctor arrived.

Ivan Ilych looks at her, scans her all over, sets against her the whiteness and plumpness and cleanness of her hands and neck, the gloss of her hair, and the sparkle of her vivacious eyes. He hates her with his whole soul. And the thrill of hatred he feels for her makes him suffer from her touch.

Her attitude towards him and his disease is still the same. Just as the doctor had adopted a certain relation to his patient which he could not abandon, so had she formed one towards him—that he was not doing something he ought to do and was himself to blame, and that she reproached him lovingly for this—and she could not now change that attitude.

"You see he doesn't listen to me and doesn't take his medicine at the proper time. And above all he lies in a position that is no doubt bad for him—with his legs up."

She described how he made Gerasim hold his legs up.

The doctor smiled with a contemptuous affability that said: "What's to be done? These sick people do have foolish fancies of that kind, but we must forgive them."

When the examination was over the doctor looked at his watch, and then Praskovya Fedorovna announced to Ivan Ilych that it was of course as he pleased, but she had sent to-day for a celebrated specialist who would examine him and have a consultation with Michael Danílovich (their regular doctor).

"Please don't raise any objections. I am doing this for my own sake," she said ironically, letting it be felt that she was doing it all for his sake and only said this to leave him no right to refuse. He remained silent, knitting his brows. He felt that he was so surrounded and involved in a mesh of falsity that it was hard to unravel anything.

Everything she did for him was entirely for her own sake, and she told him she was doing for herself what she actually was doing for herself, as if that was so incredible that he must understand the opposite.

At half-past eleven the celebrated specialist arrived. Again the sounding began and the significant conversations in his presence and in another room, about the kidneys and the appendix, and the questions and answers, with such an air of importance that again, instead of the real question of life and death which now alone confronted him, the question arose of the kidney and appendix which were not behaving as they ought to and would now be attacked by Michael Danilovich and the specialist and forced to amend their ways.

The celebrated specialist took leave of him with a serious though not hopeless look, and in reply to the timid question Ivan Ilych, with eyes glistening with fear and hope, put to him as to whether there was a chance of recovery, said that he could not vouch for it but there was a possibility. The look of hope with which Ivan Ilych watched the doctor out was so pathetic that Praskovya Fedorovna, seeing it, even wept as she left the room to hand the doctor his fee.

The gleam of hope kindled by the doctor's encouragement did not last long. The same room, the same pictures, curtains, wall-paper, medicine bottles, were all there, and the same aching suffering body, and Ivan Ilych began to moan. They gave him a subcutaneous injection and he sank into oblivion.

It was twilight when he came to. They brought him his dinner and he swallowed some beef tea with difficulty, and then everything was the same again and night was coming on.

After dinner, at seven o'clock, Praskovya Fedorovna came into the room in evening dress, her full bosom pushed up by her corset, and with traces of powder on her face. She had reminded him in the morning that they were going to the theatre. Sarah Bernhardt was visiting the town and they had a box, which he had insisted on their taking. Now he had forgotten about it and her toilet offended him, but he concealed his vexation when he remembered that he had himself insisted on their securing a box and going because it would be an instructive and aesthetic pleasure for the children.

Praskovya Fedorovna came in, self-satisfied but yet with a rather guilty air. She sat down and asked how he was, but, as he saw, only for the sake of asking and not in order to learn about it, knowing that there was nothing to learn—and then went on to what she really wanted to say: that she would not on any account have gone but that the box had been taken and Helen and their daughter were going, as well as Petrishchev (the examining magistrate, their daughter's fiancé) and that it was out of the question to let them go alone; but that she would have much preferred to sit with him for a while; and he must be sure to follow the doctor's orders while she was away.

"Oh, and Fëdor Petróvich" (the fiancé) "would like to come in. May he? And Lisa?"

"All right."

Their daughter came in in full evening dress, her fresh young flesh exposed (making a show of that very flesh which in his own case caused so much suffering), strong, healthy, evidently in love, and impatient with illness, suffering, and death, because they interfered with her happiness.

Fedor Petrovich came in too, in evening dress, his hair curled *à la Capoul*, a tight stiff collar round his long sinewy neck, an enormous white shirt-front and narrow black trousers tightly stretched over his strong thighs. He had one white glove tightly drawn on, and was holding his opera hat in his hand.

Following him the schoolboy crept in unnoticed, in a new uniform, poor little fellow, and wearing gloves. Terribly dark shadows showed under his eyes, the meaning of which Ivan Ilych knew well.

His son had always seemed pathetic to him, and now it was dreadful to see the boy's frightened look of pity. It seemed to Ivan Ilych that Vásya was the only one besides Gerasim who understood and pitied him.

They all sat down and again asked how he was. A silence followed. Lisa asked her mother about the opera-glasses, and there was an altercation between mother and daughter as to who had taken them and where they had been put. This occasioned some unpleasantness.

Fedor Petrovich inquired of Ivan Ilych whether he had ever seen Sarah Bernhardt. Ivan Ilych did not at first catch the question, but then replied: "No, have you seen her before?"

"Yes, in *Adrienne Lecouvreur*."

Praskovya Fedorovna mentioned some rôles in which Sarah Bernhardt was particularly good. Her daughter disagreed. Conversation sprang up as to the elegance and realism of her acting—the sort of conversation that is always repeated and is always the same.

In the midst of the conversation Fedor Petrovich glanced at Ivan Ilych and became silent. The others also looked at him and grew silent. Ivan Ilych was staring with glittering eyes straight before him, evidently indignant with them. This had to be rectified, but it was impossible to do so. The silence had to be broken, but for a time no one dared to break it and they all became afraid that the conventional deception would suddenly become obvious and the truth become plain to all. Lisa was the first to pluck up courage and break that silence, but by trying to hide what everybody was feeling, she betrayed it.

"Well, if we are going it's time to start," she said, looking at her watch, a present from her father, and with a faint and significant smile at Fedor Petrovich relating to something known only to them. She got up with a rustle of her dress.

They all rose, said good-night, and went away.

When they had gone it seemed to Ivan Ilych that he felt better; the falsity had gone with them. But the pain remained—that same pain and that same fear that made everything monotonously alike, nothing harder and nothing easier. Everything was worse.

Again minute followed minute and hour followed hour. Everything remained the same and there was no cessation. And the inevitable end of it all became more and more terrible.

"Yes, send Gerasim here," he replied to a question Peter asked.

IX

His wife returned late at night. She came in on tiptoe, but he heard her, opened his eyes, and made haste to close them again. She wished to send Gerasim away and to sit with him herself, but he opened his eyes and said: "No, go away."

"Are you in great pain?"

"Always the same."

"Take some opium."

He agreed and took some. She went away.

Till about three in the morning he was in a state of stupefied misery. It seemed to him that he and his pain were being thrust into a narrow, deep black sack, but though they were pushed further and further in they could not be pushed to the bottom. And this, terrible enough in itself, was accompanied by suffering. He was frightened yet wanted to fall through the sack, he struggled but yet co-operated. And suddenly he broke through, fell, and regained consciousness. Gerasim was sitting at the foot of the bed dozing quietly and patiently, while he himself lay with his emaciated stockinged legs resting on Gerasim's shoulders; the same shaded candle was there and the same unceasing pain.

"Go away, Gerasim," he whispered.

"It's all right, sir. I'll stay a while."

"No. Go away."

He removed his legs from Gerasim's shoulders, turned sideways onto his arm, and felt sorry for himself. He only waited till Gerasim had gone into the next room and then restrained himself no longer but wept like a child. He wept on account of his helplessness, his terrible loneliness, the cruelty of man, the cruelty of God, and the absence of God.

"Why hast Thou done all this? Why hast Thou brought me here? Why, why dost Thou torment me so terribly?"

He did not expect an answer and yet wept because there was no answer and could be none. The pain again grew more acute, but he did not stir and did not call. He said to himself: "Go on! Strike me! But what is it for? What have I done to Thee? What is it for?"

Then he grew quiet and not only ceased weeping but even held his breath and became all attention. It was as though he were listening not to an audible voice but to the voice of his soul, to the current of thoughts arising within him.

"What is it you want?" was the first clear conception capable of expression in words, that he heard.

"What do you want? What do you want?" he repeated to himself.

"What do I want? To live and not to suffer," he answered.

And again he listened with such concentrated attention that even his pain did not distract him.

"To live? How?" asked his inner voice.

"Why, to live as I used to—well and pleasantly."

"As you lived before, well and pleasantly?" the voice repeated.

And in imagination he began to recall the best moments of his pleasant life. But strange to say none of those best moments of his pleasant life now seemed at all what they had then seemed—none of them except the first recollections of childhood. There, in childhood, there had been something really pleasant with which it would be possible to live if it could return. But the child who had experienced that happiness existed no longer, it was like a reminiscence of somebody else.

As soon as the period began which had produced the present Ivan Ilych, all that had then seemed joys now melted before his sight and turned into something trivial and often nasty.

And the further he departed from childhood and the nearer he came to the present the more worthless and doubtful were the joys. This began with the School of Law. A little that was really good was still found there—there was light-heartedness, friendship, and hope. But in the upper classes there had already been fewer of such good moments. Then during the first years of his official career, when he was in the service of the Governor, some pleasant moments again occurred: they were the memories of love for a woman. Then all became confused and there was still less of what was good; later on again there was still less that was good, and the further he went the less there was. His marriage, a mere accident, then the disenchantment that followed it, his wife's bad breath and the sensuality and hypocrisy: then that deadly official life and those preoccupations about money, a year of it, and two, and ten, and twenty, and always the same thing. And the longer it lasted the more deadly it became. "It is as if I had been going downhill while I imagined I was going up. And that is really what it was. I was going up in public opinion, but to the same extent life was ebbing away from me. And now it is all done and there is only death."

"Then what does it mean? Why? It can't be that life is so senseless and horrible. But if it really has been so horrible and senseless, why must I die and die in agony? There is something wrong!"

"Maybe I did not live as I ought to have done," it suddenly occurred to him. "But how could that be, when I did everything properly?" he replied, and immediately dismissed from his mind this, the sole solution of all the riddles of life and death, as something quite impossible.

"Then what do you want now? To live? Live how? Live as you lived in the law courts when the usher proclaimed 'The judge is coming!' The judge is coming, the judge!" he repeated to himself. "Here he is, the judge. But I am not guilty!" he exclaimed angrily. "What is it for?" And he ceased crying, but turning his face to the wall continued to ponder on the same question: Why, and for what purpose, is there all this horror? But however much he pondered he found no answer. And whenever the thought occurred to him, as it often did, that it all resulted from his not having lived as he ought to have done, he at once recalled the correctness of his whole life and dismissed so strange an idea.

X

Another fortnight passed. Ivan Ilych now no longer left his sofa. He would not lie in bed but lay on the sofa, facing the wall nearly all the time. He suffered ever the same unceasing agonies and in his loneliness pondered always on the same insoluble question: "What is this? Can it be that it is Death?" And the inner voice answered: "Yes, it is Death."

"Why these sufferings?" And the voice answered, "For no reason—they just are so." Beyond and besides this there was nothing.

From the very beginning of his illness, ever since he had first been to see the doctor, Ivan Ilych's life had been divided between two contrary and alternating moods: now it was despair and the expectation of this uncomprehended and terrible death, and now hope and an intently interested observation of the functioning of his organs. Now before his eyes there was only a kidney or an intestine that temporarily evaded its duty, and now only that incomprehensible and dreadful death from which it was impossible to escape.

These two states of mind had alternated from the very beginning of his illness, but the further it progressed the more doubtful and fantastic became the conception of the kidney, and the more real the sense of impending death.

He had but to call to mind what he had been three months before and what he was now, to call to mind with what regularity he had been going downhill, for every possibility of hope to be shattered.

Latterly during that loneliness in which he found himself as he lay facing the back of the sofa, a loneliness in the midst of a populous town and surrounded by numerous acquaintances and relations but that yet could not have been more complete anywhere—either at the bottom of the sea or under the earth—during that terrible loneliness Ivan Ilych had lived only in memories of the past. Pictures of his past rose before him one after another. They always began with what was nearest in time and then went back to what was most remote—to his childhood—and rested there. If he thought of the stewed prunes that had been offered him that day, his mind went back to the raw shrivelled French plums of his childhood, their peculiar flavour and the flow of saliva when he sucked their stones, and along with the memory of that taste came a whole series of memories of those days: his nurse, his brother, and their toys. "No, I mustn't think of that. . . . It is too painful," Ivan Ilych said to himself, and brought himself back to the present—to the button on the back of the sofa and the creases in its morocco. "Morocco is expensive, but it does not wear well: there had been a quarrel about it. It was a different kind of quarrel and a different kind of morocco that time when we tore father's portfolio and were punished, and mamma brought us some tarts. . . ." And again his thoughts dwelt on his childhood, and again it was painful and he tried to banish them and fix his mind on something else.

Then again together with that chain of memories another series passed through his mind—of how his illness had progressed and grown worse. There also the further back he looked the more life there had been. There had been more of what was good in life and more of life itself. The two merged together. "Just as the pain went on getting worse and worse, so my life grew worse and worse," he thought. "There is one bright spot there at the back, at the beginning of life, and afterwards all becomes blacker and blacker and proceeds more and more rapidly—in inverse ratio to the square of the distance from death," thought Ivan Ilych. And the example of a stone falling downwards with increasing velocity entered his mind. Life, a series of increasing sufferings, flies further and further towards its end—the most terrible suffering. "I am flying. . . ." He shuddered, shifted himself, and tried to resist, but was already aware that resistance was impossible, and again with eyes weary of gazing but unable to cease seeing what was before them, he stared at the back of the sofa and waited—awaiting that dreadful fall and shock and destruction.

"Resistance is impossible!" he said to himself. "If I could only understand what it is all for! But that too is impossible. An explanation would be possible if it could be said that I have not lived as I ought to. But it is impossible to say that," and he remembered all the legality, correctitude, and propriety of his life. "That at any rate can certainly not be admitted," he thought, and his lips smiled ironically as if someone could see that smile and be taken in by it. "There is no explanation! Agony, death. . . . What for?"

XI

Another two weeks went by in this way and during that fortnight an event occurred that Ivan Ilych and his wife had desired. Petrishchev formally proposed. It happened in the evening. The next day Praskovya Fedorovna came into her husband's room considering how best to inform him of it, but that very night there had been a fresh change for the worse in his condition. She found him still lying on the sofa but in a different position. He lay on his back, groaning and staring fixedly straight in front of him.

She began to remind him of his medicines, but he turned his eyes towards her with such a look that she did not finish what she was saying; so great an animosity, to her in particular, did that look express.

"For Christ's sake let me die in peace!" he said.

She would have gone away, but just then their daughter came in and went up to say good morning. He looked at her as he had done at his wife, and in reply to her inquiry about his health said dryly that he would soon free them all of himself. They were both silent and after sitting with him for a while went away.

"Is it our fault?" Lisa said to her mother. "It's as if we were to blame! I am sorry for papa, but why should we be tortured?"

The doctor came at his usual time. Ivan Ilych answered "Yes" and "No," never taking his angry eyes from him, and at last said: "You know you can do nothing for me, so leave me alone."

"We can ease your sufferings."

"You can't even do that. Let me be."

The doctor went into the drawing-room and told Praskovya Fedorovna that the case was very serious and that the only resource left was opium to allay her husband's sufferings, which must be terrible.

It was true, as the doctor said, that Ivan Ilych's physical sufferings were terrible, but worse than the physical sufferings were his mental sufferings which were his chief torture.

His mental sufferings were due to the fact that that night, as he looked at Gerasim's sleepy, good-natured face with its prominent cheek-bones, the question suddenly occurred to him: "What if my whole life has really been wrong?"

It occurred to him that what had appeared perfectly impossible before, namely that he had not spent his life as he should have done, might after all be true. It occurred to him that his scarcely perceptible attempts to struggle against what was considered good by the most highly placed people, those scarcely noticeable impulses which he had immediately suppressed, might have been the real thing, and all the rest false. And his professional duties and the whole arrangement of his life and of his family, and all his social and official interests, might all have been false. He tried to defend all those things to himself and suddenly felt the weakness of what he was defending. There was nothing to defend.

"But if that is so," he said to himself, "and I am leaving this life with the consciousness that I have lost all that was given me and it is impossible to rectify it—what then?"

He lay on his back and began to pass his life in review in quite a new way. In the morning when he saw first his footman, then his wife, then his daughter, and then the doctor, their every word and movement confirmed to him the awful truth that had been revealed to him during the night. In them he saw himself—all that for which he had lived—and saw clearly that it was not real at all, but a terrible and huge deception which had hidden both life and death. This consciousness intensified his physical suffering tenfold. He groaned and tossed about, and pulled at his clothing which choked and stifled him. And he hated them on that account.

He was given a large dose of opium and became unconscious, but at noon his sufferings began again. He drove everybody away and tossed from side to side.

His wife came to him and said:

"Jean, my dear, do this for me. It can't do any harm and often helps. Healthy people often do it."

He opened his eyes wide.

"What? Take communion? Why? It's unnecessary! However. . . ."

She began to cry.

"Yes, do, my dear. I'll send for our priest. He is such a nice man."

"All right. Very well," he muttered.

When the priest came and heard his confession, Ivan Ilych was softened and seemed to feel a relief from his doubts and consequently from his sufferings, and for a moment there came a ray of hope. He again began to think of the vermiform appendix and the possibility of correcting it. He received the sacrament with tears in his eyes.

When they laid him down again afterwards he felt a moment's ease, and the hope that he might live awoke in him again. He began to think of the operation that had been suggested to him. "To live! I want to live!" he said to himself.

His wife came in to congratulate him after his communion, and when uttering the usual conventional words she added:

"You feel better, don't you?"

Without looking at her he said "Yes."

Her dress, her figure, the expression of her face, the tone of her voice, all revealed the same thing. "This is wrong, it is not as it should be. All you have lived for and still live for is falsehood and deception, hiding life and death from you." And as soon as he admitted that thought, his hatred and his agonizing physical suffering again sprang up, and with that suffering a consciousness of the unavoidable, approaching end. And to this was added a new sensation of grinding shooting pain and a feeling of suffocation.

The expression of his face when he uttered that "yes" was dreadful. Having uttered it, he looked her straight in the eyes, turned on his face with a rapidity extraordinary in his weak state and shouted:

"Go away! Go away and leave me alone!"

XII

From that moment the screaming began that continued for three days, and was so terrible that one could not hear it through two closed doors without horror. At the moment he answered his wife he realized that he was lost, that there was no return, that the end had come, the very end, and his doubts were still unsolved and remained doubts.

"Oh! Oh! Oh!" he cried in various intonations. He had begun by screaming "I won't!" and continued screaming on the letter "o."

For three whole days, during which time did not exist for him, he struggled in that black sack into which he was being thrust by an invisible, resistless force. He struggled as a man condemned to death struggles in the hands of the executioner, knowing that he cannot save himself. And every moment he felt that despite all his efforts he was drawing nearer and nearer to what terrified him. He felt that his agony was due to his being thrust into that black hole and still more to his not being able to get right into it. He was hindered from getting into it by his conviction that his life had been a good one. That very justification of his life held him fast and prevented his moving forward, and it caused him most torment of all.

Suddenly some force struck him in the chest and side, making it still harder to breathe, and he fell through the hole and there at the bottom was a light. What had happened to him was like the sensation one sometimes experiences in a railway carriage when one thinks one is going backwards while one is really going forwards and suddenly becomes aware of the real direction.

"Yes, it was all not the right thing," he said to himself, "but that's no matter. It can be done. But what *is* the right thing?" he asked himself, and suddenly grew quiet.

This occurred at the end of the third day, two hours before his death. Just then his schoolboy son had crept softly in and gone up to the bedside. The dying man was still screaming desperately and waving his arms. His hand fell on the boy's head, and the boy caught it, pressed it to his lips, and began to cry.

At that very moment Ivan Ilych fell through and caught sight of the light, and it was revealed to him that though his life had not been what it should have been, this could still be rectified. He asked himself, "What *is* the right thing?" and grew still, listening. Then he felt that someone was kissing his hand. He opened his eyes, looked at his son, and felt sorry for him. His wife came up to him and he glanced at her. She was gazing at him open-mouthed, with undried tears on her nose and cheek and a despairing look on her face. He felt sorry for her too.

"Yes, I am making them wretched," he thought. "They are sorry, but it will be better for them when I die." He wished to say this but had not the strength to utter it. "Besides, why speak? I must act," he thought. With a look at his wife he indicated his son and said: "Take him away . . . sorry for him . . . sorry for you too. . . ." He tried to add, "forgive me," but said "forego" and waved his hand, knowing that He whose understanding mattered would understand.

And suddenly it grew clear to him that what had been oppressing him and would not leave him was all dropping away at once from two sides, from ten sides, and from all sides. He was sorry for them, he must act so as not to hurt them: release them and free himself from these sufferings. "How good and how simple!" he thought. "And the pain?" he asked himself. "What has become of it? Where are you, pain?"

He turned his attention to it.

"Yes, here it is. Well, what of it? Let the pain be."

"And death . . . where is it?"

He sought his former accustomed fear of death and did not find it. "Where is it? What death?" There was no fear because there was no death.

In place of death there was light.

"So that's what it is!" he suddenly exclaimed aloud. "What joy!"

To him all this happened in a single instant, and the meaning of that instant did not change. For those present his agony continued for another two hours. Something rattled in his throat, his emaciated body twitched, then the gasping and rattle became less and less frequent.

"It is finished!" said someone near him.

He heard these words and repeated them in his soul.

"Death is finished," he said to himself. "It is no more!"

He drew in a breath, stopped in the midst of a sigh, stretched out, and died.

The Kreutzer Sonata

CHAPTER I
PASSENGERS

IT WAS EARLY SPRING. We had passed two weary days and a night in the train. Passengers riding for short distances were continually coming in and getting out, but there were three others besides myself who had come the whole way from the terminus at which the train had started: a lady, no longer young or attractive, addicted to smoking, attired in a man's great-coat, and wearing a little soft hat on her head, and whose face spoke of long and profound suffering; an acquaintance of hers, a talkative gentleman of forty, faultlessly attired in brand-new clothes; and another gentleman, short of stature, and of fitful, nervous movements, not yet old, although his curly hair was prematurely gray. His eyes wandered rapidly from object to object as he sat aloof from all the other passengers.

He wore an old great-coat made evidently by an expensive tailor, with Astrakhan collar and Astrakhan cap to match. Underneath his great-coat, when unbuttoned, a jacket could be seen and an embroidered shirt, of the kind known as "Russian" shirts. It was characteristic of this person that he uttered from time to time peculiar sounds resembling short coughs or laughter just begun and suddenly broken off. During the journey he sedulously avoided making the acquaintance of, or communicating with, his fellow-passengers: to all their attempts at conversation he gave curt and churlish replies, and would either take to reading or to smoking, looking out through the window in the latter case, or else would draw forth his provisions from an old bag and make tea for himself, or eat a little. It seemed to me that his loneliness oppressed him, and I made more than one effort to enter into conversation with him, but each time our eyes met—and it happened pretty frequently, for he sat on the further end of the seat opposite to me—he always turned away, burying himself in his book or looking out through the window.

During the stop we made at a large station on the evening of the second day, this nervous passenger went out to fetch boiling water to make himself some tea. The gentleman with the brand-new clothes—a lawyer, as I afterward gathered—went to the refreshment-room to have tea with the lady smoker in the man's great-coat. While they were away several new passengers entered the carriage, among them a tall, clean-shaven old man—evidently a merchant—his face full of the wrinkles of age, wearing an ample fur coat, made from the skins of American skunks, and a cloth cap with a huge peak. He sat down on the seat opposite to that occupied by the lady and the lawyer, and without more ado entered into a conversation with a young man, apparently a merchant's clerk, who had got in at this same station.

I was sitting on the further end of the seat opposite, and, as the train was standing still, I could distinguish snatches of their conversation, whenever there was no one walking along the passage. The merchant began by volunteering the information that he was bound for his estate, situated close by the next station. Then they spoke, as is always done in such cases, about prices, about trade, discussed the state of business in Moscow at that moment, and then went on to talk of the Fair of Nischny Novgorod. The clerk began to describe the drinking bouts and other wild pranks of a well-known rich merchant at the fair, but the old man did not allow him to tell his story to the end, but interrupted him with tales of revelries of by-gone times at the Fair of Kunavin, in which he himself took part. He took evident pride in his participation in these saturnalia, and with visible delight went on to relate how he and that same rich merchant had once in Kunavin, under the influence of liquor, played such a trick that it could not even be described otherwise than in a whisper; it made the clerk, when he heard it, roar with laughter till his voice resounded from one end of the carriage to the other, the old man also laughing the while and displaying two yellow teeth. Not expecting to hear anything interesting, I arose and moved toward the door with the intention of walking to and fro on the platform till the departure of the train. On the threshold I met the lawyer and the lady engaged in a lively conversation on their way back to their places. "You'll not have time," exclaimed the communicative lawyer, addressing me; "the second bell is about to be rung this moment."

And he was right. Scarcely had I reached the end of the train, when the second bell was rung. I returned and found the lawyer and the lady continuing their lively discussion. The old merchant seated opposite them was looking straight before him, occasionally pursing his lips disapprovingly. "Then she told her husband right out," the lawyer said, with a smile, as I was moving past him to my seat, "that she could not and would not live with him any longer, inasmuch as . . ." The rest of the story I could not catch, for no sooner had I taken my place than other passengers came in; then the guard entered; soon afterward a luggage porter rushed in, and for a considerable time such a noise was kept up, that I could not hear the conversation.

When the din had subsided, and the lawyer's voice again became audible, I noticed that the conversation had taken a new turn, and, from being private, had drifted into general topics. The lawyer was remarking that the question of divorce was now claiming and receiving the serious attention of the public in all Europe, and that even in Russia the cases in which it was granted were growing more and more frequent. Becoming suddenly aware that his was the only voice heard in the carriage, he ceased speaking, and turning to the old man: "In old times there was nothing like that, I am sure, was there?" he said, blandly, smiling. The merchant was about to make some reply, but at this moment the train started, and, taking off his cap, he began to make the sign of the cross, and to mutter his prayers in a low whisper. The lawyer, turning away his eyes, courteously waited till he had done. Having finished his prayer and crossed himself three times, the old man put his cap on, pressed it well on his head, made himself comfortable in his seat, and then began to speak.

"It used to happen in old times, too, sir," he observed, "only not so often as it does now. But at present it could not be otherwise than it is. People have become so surprisingly enlightened."

The train, moving faster and faster, groaned and clanked, and made it very difficult for me to hear what was being said, and, as the conversation interested me, I moved nearer to the speakers. My neighbor, the nervous passenger with the glowing eyes, was also, I could see, interested; and he, too, made a visible effort to catch what was being said, but without rising or leaving his place.

"In what respect is education an evil?" asked the lady, with a scarcely perceptible smile on her lips. "Surely it can not be contended that it is better to marry as they did in old times, the bride and bridegroom not having as much as seen each other before the wedding?" she continued, after the manner of many ladies, replying not to the words of her interlocutor but to the remarks which she supposed he would make. "They did not know whether they liked each other, whether they could possibly like each other, and yet they married they knew not whom, making themselves miserable for all their lives. And yet that is a better state of things, in your opinion?" she went on, unmistakably addressing her remarks to the lawyer and myself, and scarcely, if at all, to the old man with whom she was ostensibly talking.

"Nowadays people have become surprisingly enlightened," repeated the merchant, contemptuously eyeing the lady and leaving her query unanswered.

"It would give me pleasure to hear how you explain the connection between education and discord in married life," exclaimed the lawyer, smiling almost imperceptibly.

The merchant was about to say something, when the lady interrupted him, saying: "No, those times are gone for good."

The lawyer, however, checked her, and exclaimed: "Pray allow him to explain his meaning!"

"Folly comes from education," cried the merchant in a dogmatic manner.

"They join in marriage people who do not love each other, and then they are astonished that such couples do not live happily," hurriedly exclaimed the lady turning round to look at the lawyer, at me, and even at the clerk, who, having risen from his place, was leaning on the back of the seat, smiling and listening to the discussion. "It is only animals that you can treat in that way," she continued, with the evident intention of stinging the merchant, "pairing and coupling them as their owner thinks fit; but men and women have their own inclinations and attachments."

"You ought not to talk in that way, ma'am," observed the merchant; "an animal is a beast, but a law has been given to man."

"Yes, but how are you to live with a man if you have no love for him?" cried the lady, apparently in haste to give utterance to thoughts which she probably believed to be very original.

"In former times no heed was given to such things," said the merchant in a solemn, peremptory manner; "it is only in our days that they have come into vogue. The moment the slightest hitch occurs, the wife bristles up with her 'I'll not live with you.' The very peasants have adopted the new fashion, and are conducting themselves accordingly. 'Here,' cries a countryman's mate, 'here, take your blouses and your drawers, I'll go off with Jack. He has a finer curly head than you have.' Talk about wonders happening after this! The first and chief thing that should be looked for in a woman is fear."

The clerk looked at the lawyer, the lady, and at me, keeping back his smile in reserve, and ready either to ridicule or to approve the merchant's discourse, according to the reception it met with.

"What kind of fear?" asked the lady.

"The kind meant by the words: 'And she shall fear her husband.' That's the kind of fear."

"Those days are long since past and gone, my good man," exclaimed the lady, with a certain touch of bitterness.

"No, ma'am, those days can not pass away. As Eve, the woman, once was created from the man's rib, so she will remain till the end of time." These words the old man uttered solemnly, shaking his head so triumphantly the while that the clerk at once decided that the victory would be on his side, and consequently he burst out laughing.

"Yes, that's the way you men reason out the question," exclaimed the lady, reluctant to surrender, and looking away from us. "You give yourselves liberty, while you want to keep us women behind bolts and bars. You take very good care, I am sure, to allow yourselves every liberty."

"Nobody accords us permission; a man, you know, brings no increase into the house by misconduct outside it. But a woman, a wife, you see, is a frail vessel."

The emphasis and gravity with which the merchant delivered himself of these judgments had evidently a powerfully persuasive effect on his hearers. Even the lady was conscious of defeat: still, however, she refused to give in.

"Yes, but I think for all that you will admit that a woman is a human being, endowed with feeling, just as a man is. Now what is she to do if she does not love her husband?"

"If she does not love her husband?" angrily repeated the merchant, moving his brows and his lips simultaneously. "Don't you fear, she'll learn to love him!"

This unlooked-for argument especially tickled the clerk's fancy, and he uttered an inarticulate sound significative of approval.

"Oh, but she will not learn to love him," declared the lady; "and if love is lacking, it is not force that can engender it."

"Well, but suppose a woman has proved unfaithful to her husband; how then?" asked the lawyer.

"That has not to be taken into account at all," replied the old man. "One should always take effective measures to prevent it."

"Yes, but suppose it should occur in spite of your measures; it's a fact that it does take place; what then?"

"Wherever else it happens, it is unknown in our circles," was the merchant's reply.

All became silent. The clerk shifted his position, moved a little nearer, and apparently not wishing to be behind the others, began with a smile as follows:

"Yes, here now is a scandalous affair that took place among our people, and a hard one to disentangle, too! She was a queer woman, a loose sort, you know. And she did go in for games, I tell you! Her husband was a well enough sort of man in his way, and had all his wits about him. She began tricks with the shop-boy. Her husband tried to bring her round, and get her to keep straight by soft talk and advice. But she wouldn't knuckle down. She did no end of queer things, that woman. She got to such a pitch that she made no bones of stealing his money. He beat her then. Well, and what do you think came of it? Why, she got worse and worse, and at last she went off with an unbaptized fellow—a Jew! Now, what was her husband to do, I ask you? He shook her off altogether; and now he's living like a bachelor, and she's going from bad to worse."

"Because he's a fool!" exclaimed the old man. "If he had put a spoke in her wheel from the very outset; if he had given her a thorough good taming, I'll go bail she'd be living with him to-day. Never let them have their way from the very beginning. 'Don't trust your horse in the field nor your wife in your home,' as the saying is."

At this point in the conversation the guard came in to collect the tickets for the next station. The old man gave up his. "Yes, sir, women must be tamed in time, or else all's lost."

"Well, but how do you reconcile that with what you yourself related a short time ago about what the men did at the Fair of Kunavin?" I asked, unable to keep silent any longer.

"Oh, that's a different thing altogether," he answered, and relapsed immediately into silence.

Shortly afterward the shrill whistle of the engine was heard, and he rose, dragged out a bag from under the seat, pulled his fur coat closer about him, and, slightly raising his cap, left the carriage to take his place on the little platform near the break.

CHAPTER II

LOVE DEFINED

SCARCELY HAD HE left the carriage when the conversation began again, several voices being heard simultaneously.

"There goes a patriarchal old grandfather!" exclaimed the clerk.

"The incarnation of tyrannical home government," ejaculated the lady. "What a barbarous conception of women and of marriage he has!"

"Yes, we are still far off from European views on marriage," observed the lawyer.

"The strangest thing of all about such people," resumed the lady, "is that they do not understand that marriage without love is not marriage at all; that the only thing that can hallow marriage is love, and that the only genuine marriage is that which is hallowed by love."

The clerk listened and smiled, desirous of impressing on his memory for future use as many enlightened remarks as possible. In the middle of the lady's talk a noise was heard as of suppressed laughter or a smothered sob, and, turning round, we beheld my neighbor, the gray-haired, lonely man with the lustrous eyes, who during the course of the conversation, which evidently interested him, had moved quite close to us, without being observed. He was standing with his arms resting on the back of the seat, and he appeared very excited, his face being quite red, and the nervous twitching of the facial muscles being painfully visible.

"What kind of love do you mean—the love that hallows marriage?" he asked, stammering.

Noticing the state of agitation in which her interlocutor addressed her, the lady put as much gentleness and thoroughness into her reply as was possible.

"Real, genuine love," she explained; "if such love exists between the man and the woman, marriage is possible."

"Yes; but what are we to understand by real, genuine love?" insisted the man with the glowing eyes, smiling awkwardly, and displaying great timidity as he put the question.

"Surely, every one knows what is meant by love!" exclaimed the lady.

"I do not," objected her questioner; "you should define what you mean by—"

"What? Why, it's very simple," replied the lady, who, nevertheless, became thoughtful and silent for a few moments. Then resuming, "What is love?" she repeated, "love is the preference of one person for another, to the exclusion of every one else."

"Preference for what period of time? For a month? For two days? Or for half an hour?" queried the passenger, with a laugh.

"No: it is clear you have something else in mind," said the lady.

"No; I am speaking of the same thing as you are."

"The lady maintains," said the advocate, interposing, "that marriage should be the outcome in the first place of an attachment (or call it love, if you will), and that if such a sentiment exists, then, and not otherwise, is marriage hallowed, so to say. In the next place, that every marriage not based upon this natural predilection (or love, if you prefer the term), is devoid of the element that makes it morally binding. Have I interpreted you aright?" he asked, turning to the lady.

The lady by a nod of her head signified her approval of the lawyer's exposition.

"In the next place—" the lawyer went on; but the nervous gentleman, with the glowing eyes, which now resembled two coals of fire, was evidently unable any longer to control himself, for breaking in on the lawyer's speech, he began:

"No, I am speaking of exactly the same thing, the predilection of one person for another, only I ask how long is this predilection to last?"

"How long? A long time, sometimes a whole life-time," answered the lady, shrugging her shoulders.

"Yes, but that is only in novels. In life it is never so. In life this predilection of one person for another lasts in very rare instances for years; generally for months, and sometimes for weeks, for days, for hours," he exclaimed, obviously conscious that he was startling us all by this expression of opinion, and satisfied that it should be so.

"Oh, how can you! No, but— Pardon me, but—" all three of us began simultaneously. Even the clerk uttered some sound of disapproval.

"Yes, I know," he exclaimed, in a high voice, "you are talking of that which is supposed to be, whereas I was speaking of that which is. Every man feels what you call love toward every pretty woman."

"Oh, that's horrible—to say such things. It is certain that there is such a sentiment as love—love that is given us not for months or years, but for our life-time. Is not that so?" asked the lady.

"Certainly not. Even if we admit that a man may conceive a predilection for a certain woman, and that it lasts all his life, it is most highly probable that the woman's predilection will be for some one else. So it has ever been, and so it will ever continue to be in this world of ours." Having delivered himself of this opinion, he took out his cigarette-case and began to smoke.

"It may be reciprocal," urged the lawyer.

"No, it can not be," he answered; "just as in a cartload of peas no two peas will lie exactly side by side. Besides, we are not dealing in this case with mere improbabilities; one of the certain elements of the question is satiation. To say that you can love one person all your life is just like saying that one candle will continue burning as long as you live." As he said this, he greedily drew in the smoke of his cigarette.

"You are speaking of another sort of love," objected the lady: "don't you admit the existence of love founded on identity of ideals, on spiritual kinship?"

"Identity of ideals!" he repeated, uttering his strange noise; "but in that case there is no reason why they should sleep together—pardon me this coarseness. The idea of people sleeping together because their ideals are identical!" and he laughed nervously.

"Allow me to point out," interposed the lawyer, "that the facts are dead against you. We see that marriages exist; that all mankind, or at least the great majority, contract matrimonial unions, and that many live honorably during a long married life."

The gray-haired passenger again laughed.

"You maintain," he said, "that marriages are based on love. But when I express my doubts as to the existence of any but physical love, you set about proving the existence of love by pointing to the existence of marriages. Marriage in our days is nothing but deceit."

"I beg your pardon," exclaimed the lawyer, "all I affirm is that marriages have existed, and do still exist."

"Marriages exist! Yes, but why do they exist? They existed and still exist among those peoples who discern something mysterious, sacramental in marriage; a sacrament which has a binding power in the sight of God. Among such people marriages do indeed subsist, but not among us. In our country people contract matrimonial unions who in marriage see nothing of the sort, and the result is deceit or violence. If deceit, it is more easily borne; the husband and wife merely deceive others, leading them to believe that they are living in real marriage, whereas they are living in polygamy and polyandry. This is bad; it is tolerable, however; but when, as is more frequently the case, husband and wife have taken upon themselves the outward obligation of living together as long as life is given them, and yet from the second month of married life already hate each other, and although eagerly desirous to separate, yet continue to live together—life at last becomes a terrible hell, from which they endeavor to escape by drinking themselves to death, blowing out their brains, poisoning and killing themselves and each other." He spoke rapidly, allowing no one to interpose a word, and grew more and more excited as he spoke.

We all remained silent, feeling ill at ease.

"Yes, undoubtedly critical episodes do occur in married life," said the lawyer, at last breaking the awkward silence with the object of putting an end to the discussion, which was becoming unduly heated.

"I see you know who I am?" said the gray-haired passenger quietly, and, as it seemed, calmly.

"No, I have not the pleasure."

"Well, the pleasure is not much. I am Pozdnischeff, the person to whom occurred that 'critical episode' to which you allude, the episode that consisted in his killing his wife," he exclaimed, looking hurriedly at each of us in turn. As none of us hit upon any remark appropriate to such an occasion, we remained silent. "Well, it's all the same," he continued, making that strange noise to which he was addicted. "Anyhow, I ask your pardon. Ah! I will not embarrass you any longer with my presence!"

"But not at all; don't mention such a thing; not at all!" exclaimed the lawyer, not exactly knowing what he meant by "not at all." Pozdnischeff, however, paid no attention to what he said, and turning round, went back to his place. The gentleman began to converse with the lady in whispers.

CHAPTER III

THE TALE OF POZDNISCHEFF

I WAS SEATED opposite Pozdnischeff, but as I could not think of anything appropriate to say to him, and as it was too dark to read, I closed my eyes and simulated a desire to sleep. We remained thus till we reached the next station, where the gentleman and lady got into another carriage, after having previously arranged the matter with the guard. The clerk, having made himself comfortable on the seat, had gone to sleep. Pozdnischeff was all the time smoking and drinking tea—the tea he had made at the previous station. No sooner did I open my eyes and look about me than he addressed me with determination in his manner and irritation in his voice:

"Perhaps it is disagreeable to you to sit near me, now that you know who I am. If so, I will go away."

"Not at all. Please don't think such a thing."

"Well, then, can I offer you some? It is somewhat strong, I fear." With this he poured me out some tea.

"They talk . . . but what they say is all lies—"

"To what are you referring?" I inquired.

"To the same subject, of course; to that love of theirs, and to its nature. You are not sleepy?"

"No; not in the least."

"Well, if you like, I'll tell you how it was that I was led by this very love to do what I did?"

"Certainly, if the effort is not too painful for you—"

"Not at all. To keep silence is painful. Have some more tea? Or is it too strong for you?"

The tea was in truth very strong; it was almost like beer; however, I drank a tumbler of it. Just then the conductor passed through the carriage; Pozdnischeff scowled at him, and did not begin till he had left.

"Well, then, I'll tell you the story. But are you really sure you care to hear it?"

I assured him that I desired it very much. He remained silent a moment, then rubbed his face with his hands and began:

"Before marriage I lived as all other men live in our social stratum. I am a land-owner, a candidate of the university, and at one time was marshal of the nobility. Until I married I lived like everybody else—that is to say, not morally—and, like men in my own walk of life, fancied that by living in this way I was performing my duty. I considered myself a model, and believed that I was a thoroughly moral man. Not being a seducer, nor possessed of depraved tastes, I did not make pleasure the main object of my life, as did many men of my own age and station. I yielded moderately, decently, for the sake of health. I avoided women who by conceiving a strong affection for me might fetter me in any way. For the rest, for aught I know, there may have been attachments, but I acted as if they did not exist. And not merely did I hold this to be moral conduct, but I was actually proud of it."

Here he stopped short and uttered that peculiar sound which he apparently always made whenever a new thought occurred to him.

"It was this," he continued, "that constituted the hideousness of my conduct. It is not anything physical that imports; what is wrong is the exemption of one's self from all moral relations when terms of intimacy exist. And it was precisely this exemption of myself from all such moral ties that I regarded as my peculiar merit. I remember how terribly I suffered once when I had failed to acknowledge, by means of a present of money, a woman who had most probably fallen in love with me. Nor did I recover my wonted tranquillity until I had forwarded her money, and thereby made it clear to her that I considered myself perfectly untrammeled by any kind of moral ties.

"You need not shake your head as if you agreed with me," he suddenly exclaimed. "I know this trick well. Every man, and you among the rest, unless you are a rare exception, shares these very views in accordance with which I acted. It's all the same, however; forgive me," he continued, "but the truth is that all this is very terrible."

"What is terrible?" I asked.

"The abyss of delusions in which we live concerning women and our relations toward them. Yes; I am unable to speak calmly of it, not because of the 'episode,' as he termed it, which occurred to me in connection therewith, but because ever since it took place my eyes have been opened, and I see things in quite a different light. Everything is turned inside out; yes, inside out."

He lighted a cigarette, and, resting his elbows on his knees, resumed. In the darkness I could not distinguish his face; I could only hear, high above the creaking and noise of the train, the sound of his impressive and agreeable voice.

CHAPTER IV

HIGH PRIEST OF SCIENCE

"YES, IT WAS only after I had been tortured and agonized, and, thanks to this torture and agony, that I understood wherein lay the root of the evil; it is only since I learned what ought to be, that I realize so fully the hideousness of that which is.

"Let me now tell you when and how those circumstances originated which led up to that terrible episode of my life. I was not quite sixteen years old when I took the first step on that fatal journey. It happened when I was still a pupil in the gymnasium, and my elder brother a freshman at the university. I had never known a woman before, but at the same time I possessed no more claim to be called an innocent boy than did any of the unfortunate children of our social stratum. For nearly two years previously my soul had been defiled by my comrades, and already the bare thought of woman, not of any particular woman, but of a woman in general, tormented me.

"My thoughts, when alone, were therefore, no longer pure. I tortured myself as ninety-nine one hundredths of our boys torture themselves. I was horrified, I was agonized, I prayed, and I fell. I had already, therefore, been corrupted in imagination. I was perishing alone, and had not as yet laid violent hands upon other human beings, in order to involve them in my ruin.

"It was at this conjuncture that one day a friend of my brother's, also a student, a gay youth, and what is commonly called a right good fellow—that is, a worthless villain—who had taught us to drink and to gamble, persuaded us one night, after a drinking bout, to go *there*. And we went. My brother was also innocent up to then, and fell on the same night. And I, a mere stripling of sixteen, fell also, not realizing what I did.

"I had never heard from any one of my elders that what I was doing was wrong. And, what is more, even now, boys of the present generation never hear it. True, it is to be found in the Decalogue, but then the Decalogue exists only to be repeated by heart at examinations in schools and universities, and even in that capacity it is not very necessary; certainly not by any means as indispensable as is the grammatical commandment that the Latin particle *ut* is to be employed in the conditional clauses of a sentence. At all events, I never heard from any of my elders, whose opinion I respected, that what I was doing was wrong. On the contrary, I heard from people whom I esteemed that I was doing quite right. I was told that, once done, all my struggles and my sufferings would disappear. This I had both heard and read. I had not been told by my elders that I was doing wrong; the men I knew regarded their conduct as a sort of heroism, as it were. So that, altogether, it was clear that it could have none but good effects. Had I any fear of evil consequences? Even that had been foreseen, and a provident government had taken thought of it. Salaried doctors are employed to look after these matters. This is as it ought to be. It is the doctors who affirm what is indispensable to good health, and it is they who sanction a system of conduct. I am personally acquainted with mothers who take measures precisely as the doctors direct in these matters. It is science that is responsible."

"Why science?" I asked.

"Who are the doctors," he answered, "if not the high priests of science? Who demoralizes our youth by affirming what is indispensable to good health? And then, with airs of unutterable self-importance, they set about curing complaints."

"And why should they not cure complaints?" I asked.

"Because if the one hundredth part of the efforts made to cure had been directed to the extirpation of indulgence, these complaints would have long ago disappeared. But no; all those efforts are put forth, not for the purpose of rooting out evil, but with the express object of encouraging it, of guaranteeing those who practice it from risks of evil accompanying it. But that is not the point I was driving at. What I wanted to emphasize is the circumstance that what happened to me is exactly what befalls nine tenths, if not more, of the members, not only of our social sphere, but of all classes and conditions of our society, not excepting even the peasants: I fell without even the excuse that I was yielding to natural love. No; it was not love that caused me to fall; I fell, simply because those persons in whose midst I lived looked upon that which constituted my fall, some as a lawful and useful action, others as a most natural, and not only excusable, but perfectly innocent amusement for a young man to engage in. As for me, I had not a suspicion that I had done anything that could be appropriately described as a fall. I simply began to give myself up to what was partly a pleasure and partly, as I was assured, a necessity, just as I had taken to drink and to smoke. And yet in this first fall there was something peculiar, something pathetic. I remember that the very instant I had fallen I was overwhelmed with sadness, and I felt that I should like to sit down and weep. Yes, I could have wept over the loss of my innocence, over the wrong I had committed, which no ages could ever wash away.

"Yes, I could never again hope to look upon woman in the simple, natural way characteristic of the pure and the innocent. Just as the opium-eater, the drunkard, and the immoderate smoker are not normal men, so is he who has fallen as I did; he is a tainted, corrupted man. As an opium-eater, or a drunkard, is readily recognizable by his face, his gait, his manner, so also is such a man as I became. He may succeed in exercising a certain self-mastery, in repressing tell-tale movements and looks that have become spontaneous—in a word, he may still struggle with himself and his proclivities, but he can never again recover those simple, clear, pure relations with womankind, relations as of a brother toward his sister.

"And I became a voluptuary, and remained one. And this it was that worked my ruin."

CHAPTER V
HER STUPEFACTION

"After this I sank deeper and deeper into the slough. And yet what I recall is what *I* did—I who was a continual butt for the scornful gibes of my comrades, owing to my relative 'innocence.' What if you were to hear of the doings of the gilded youth, of army officers, of 'Parisians'! And yet all these persons, myself included, when we were profligates of thirty years of age, our souls laden with hundreds of multiform crimes, how often have we entered the salon or the ballroom, spruce and neat, washed, shaved, perfumed in spotless linen and irreproachable evening dress or faultless uniform—as emblems of purity! How charming!

"Just reflect for a moment upon what ought to be, and confront it with what really is. What ought to be is this: when a person of this description in society approaches my sister or my daughter, I, knowing his life, should walk up to him, draw him aside, and, addressing him in a whisper, say: 'Friend, I know the kind of life you lead, how you spend your nights and with whom. This is no fit place for you. Here there are spotless innocent girls. Withdraw!' This is what ought to take place. What really does occur is this: when such a person makes his appearance and dances with my sister or my daughter, encircling her waist with his arm, we laugh at it if he is rich and has powerful friends. Oh, abomination! How long shall we have to wait for the time when this execrable state of things, this tissue of damnable lies, will be finally shown up and exploded?"

He again made those peculiar sounds of his several times in succession, and again took tea. The tea, I must say, was extremely strong, and there was no water at hand with which to weaken it. I felt extremely stimulated by the two glasses of it that I had drunk. It doubtlessly affected him, too, in a similar way, for the more tea he drank the more excited he grew. His voice became more and more sonorous and expressive; he was continually changing his position, and now putting on his cap, now taking it off; and his face seemed to undergo strange transfigurations in the gathering darkness.

"In this way I lived," he resumed, "till I was thirty years of age, never for a single moment giving up my intention to marry, settle down, and lead the purest and most ideal family life conceivable. With this object in view, I carefully sought for a suitable young girl. I looked around with critical gaze in search of a girl whose purity would qualify her to aspire to the dignity of becoming my wife. I slighted and rejected several because, forsooth, they were not immaculate enough for me. At last, however, my search was successful: I discovered a person whom I regarded as worthy of myself.

"She was one of two daughters of a land-owner of Penza, once a wealthy man, but at that time ruined and in straitened circumstances. One evening she and I had been out boating together, and when night came on, and we were returning home, lighted by the soft rays of the moon, and I sat side by side with her, admiring her bewitching curls and her well-shaped figure, becomingly set off in a well-fitting jersey, I suddenly decided that she was the person. I fancied that night that she comprehended everything that I felt and thought, and that what I felt and thought was sublime to a degree. In truth, at the root of this fancy lay her curls and her jersey, which became her remarkably well, and the desire for greater proximity.

"What a strange illusion it is to suppose that beauty is goodness! A beautiful woman utters absurdities; we listen and we hear not the absurdities, but wise thoughts. She speaks, she does odious things, and yet we are only conscious of something agreeable. If she refrains from absurd or hateful words and acts, and if she is beautiful to boot, we are straightway convinced that she is a paragon of wisdom and morality. As for me, I returned home in ecstasies, deciding that she was the pink of moral perfection, and for this reason worthy to be my wife. The next day I proposed for her.

"What an absurd entanglement of ideas! Out of a thousand men who marry, not only in our social sphere, but also unfortunately in the rank of the people, there is scarcely one who has not, like Don Juan, been married before innumerable times. (True, there are now, I hear, and I have personal experience of what I say, pure young men who feel and know that purity is no laughing matter, but a most important affair. May God succor them! But in my time there was not one such in ten thousand.) Everybody is perfectly well aware that this is the normal state of things, and yet everybody feigns to believe that it is entirely different.

"All novels are full of detailed descriptions of the feelings of their heroes, and the appearance of the lakes and trees round which they ramble. But when their love for a young girl is touched upon, no mention whatever is made about the previous experiences of the interesting hero. Or if such novels exist, they are never put in the hands of the persons most concerned to know these things—namely, young girls. At first a pretense is made to girls that the wickedness which fills up half the life of a man in our cities and villages does not exist at all. In time we grow so accustomed to this hypocrisy that we honestly begin to believe that we are all moral people and live in a moral world. Girls, poor things, believe this quite seriously. It was also the conviction of my unfortunate wife. Once before our marriage I showed her my diary containing entries from which she could gain a glimpse of certain episodes of my former life, especially of my last *liaison*, which I felt it advisable to bring to her knowledge, lest it should be communicated to her by others. I well recollect the horror, the despair, the stupefaction which she felt when she knew and understood what had taken place. I saw that she wanted to break off all relations with me then and there."

"And what prevented her from breaking off?" I queried.

He uttered again the peculiar sound of his, remained silent, and drank a little tea.

"Anyhow, it is better so, yes, it is better so," he exclaimed. "It serves me right."

CHAPTER VI
DECEIVED DAUGHTERS

"BUT THAT IS not the point. What I wanted to say is that the only persons who are really deceived in all this are the unfortunate girls. The mothers, initiated by their husbands, see through it all, and, while simulating belief in the purity of men, act in a manner wholly incompatible with such a belief. They know with what bait to catch men for themselves and for their daughters.

"It is only we men who do not know this, and we are ignorant of it simply because we do not wish to know. Women are well aware that what is commonly called sublime and poetical love depends not upon moral qualities, but on frequent meetings, and on the style in which the hair is done up, and on the color and cut of the dress. Ask an experienced coquette eagerly bent upon captivating a man, which of the two risks she would rather incur: that of being convicted of deceit, cruelty, or even of immoral conduct in presence of the man whom she is endeavoring to attract, or of appearing before him in a badly made and ugly dress. She will unhesitatingly prefer the first. For she well knows that men are continually lying about lofty sentiments; that what they really want is only the woman herself and that they consequently freely condone every species of bad conduct, while they will never forgive a dress that is badly cut, tastelessly trimmed, or suggestive of *mauvais ton.*[1] Every coquette is keenly conscious of this; every innocent girl is unconsciously aware of this: Hence these odious jerseys and projections behind, these exposed shoulders, arms, and almost open breasts. Women, particularly those who have passed through the masculine school, are alive to the fact that conversations on lofty themes are mere hollow phrases; that the object of a man's desire is the person, and whatever sets that out in its most seductive light; and they act in strict accordance with this knowledge.

"If we could only throw aside that familiarity with shocking conventions which has become second nature to us, and look at life among the higher classes as it really is, we should find it absolutely shameful. You don't agree with me? I will prove it to you," he said, interrupting me. "You maintain that women of our social sphere live for interests other than those which play a part in the life of lost women, but I tell you that it is not so, and I will make good my contention.

"If people wholly differ in their aims of life, in the significance they ascribe to human existence, this divergence will be assuredly reflected in their outward conduct; and their external appearance will be as different as are their views. Look now upon the unfortunate and despised sisterhood of fallen women and compare them with the ladies of the highest society. What do you observe? The same toilets, the same costumes, the same perfumes, the same exposure of the arms and shoulders, the same projections behind, the same passion for jewelry, for costly glittering ornaments, the same amusements, dances, music, and song. And as the former class of women employ all of these things for the purposes of seduction, so also do the latter. There is absolutely no difference between them."

[1] [Unfashionableness.]

CHAPTER VII
CONTRIVED PASSION

"IT WAS THUS, then, that I was caught by these jerseys, curls, and projections. It was easy to catch me, seeing that I had been brought up under conditions calculated to breed young lovers, somewhat as cucumbers are forced in hot-houses. Consider our stimulating, superfluous food, combined as it is with complete physical inactivity.

"You may wonder or not wonder, just as you like, but so it is. I myself did not discover this till very lately. And it causes me profound suffering to reflect that nobody is aware of it now, and that people utter in consequence such absurdities as those to which that lady here gave expression a short time ago.

"Last spring a number of peasants were working in our neighborhood on a railway embankment. The usual food of a strong peasant when engaged in light field labor consists of bread (kvass), onions, and this keeps him alive, active, and healthy. When he enters into the service of a railway company his food is porridge, and a pound of meat daily. This meat he gives out again in the form of sixteen hours' labor, driving a wheelbarrow of thirty poods, which is just as much as he is able to perform. We, on the other hand, eat game, meat, and fish, besides sundry other kinds of heat-giving food and drink. Now where, may I ask, does all this go? To produce excesses, abnormal excitement, which, passing through the prism of our artificial life, assumes the form of falling in love.

"Thus I fell in love, as all men do, and none of the characteristic traits of that state were wanting. Ecstasies, tenderness, and poetry were all there, in appearance at least, but in reality my love was the result of the contrivances of the mamma and the dressmaker on the one hand, and good dinners and inactivity on the other. If, on the one hand, there had been no boating excursions, no dress-makers to arrange wasp-like waists, and so on; had my wife been dressed in a plain gown and stayed at home; and if, on the other hand, I had been leading a normal life, I should not have fallen in love, and all that took place subsequently and in consequence of that, would never have occurred."

CHAPTER VIII
TAKE MY LILY!

"As it was, however, my frame of mind, the becoming dress, and the rowing in the boat, contributed to make the thing a success. Twenty times over it had failed before; this time it succeeded, and I fell into what may be described as a kind of trap.

"I am not joking when I say that marriages in our days are arranged like traps. What is there natural about them? A girl grows up and must be married. It seems a very simple problem on the face of it, especially if she is not a scarecrow, and there is a sufficiency of men desirous of marrying. In old times it was very plain sailing. The girl became of age, and the parents arranged the match. It is still so with the Chinese, Indians, Mohammedans, the lower orders of Russians; in a word, with ninety-nine hundredths of all mankind. It remained for the one hundredth part or even less of debased humanity to make the discovery that this was not the proper way of solving the problem and to devise a new method. Now, what are the essential characteristics of this new system? The girls sit at home and the young men go, as it were, to the market, and choose them, the girls anxiously waiting and thinking, but not daring to say plainly, 'Pray take me, dear! No, take me. Not her, but me, please. Look what shoulders I have got!' And we men, meanwhile, walk up and down, scrutinizing them and feeling perfectly satisfied, each one saying to himself, 'I know, forsooth, that I shall not be taken in.' And so we stroll backward and forward, delighted that everything is so nicely arranged for us, when suddenly one of us trips up, falls, and is caught in the trap."

"Well, but what would you have?" I asked. "Surely you would not wish the girls to propose to the men?"

"I really do not know what I would have, I only feel that if there is to be equality, let there be real equality.

"If match-making by professional match-makers is found to be debasing, our system is a thousand times more degrading, for in the former case the rights and chances are equal on both sides, whereas in the latter the woman is either a slave in the market or a mere decoy.

"Tell a mother or her daughter the plain truth, namely, that all her efforts are directed to the one end of catching a husband. Heavens! what an insult that would be! And yet they all do this, and there is nothing else for them to do; it is peculiarly harrowing to see sometimes very young, poor, innocent girls occupied in this way. Lamentable as all this is, if it were, at least, done openly, above board, it would be different, but as a matter of fact it is all deceit.

" 'Ah! "The Origin of Species"—how interesting!' a mamma would exclaim. 'Oh, Lily is very much interested in painting!' 'And you, do you propose going to the exhibition?' 'How instructive!' 'Driving in a drosky!'[1] 'The play!' 'The concert!' 'Ah! how wonderful!' 'Lily is simply wild about music!' 'And you, how is it that you do not share these convictions?' 'Boating parties!—ah! boating parties!'

"The thought underlying all these ejaculations is one and the same. Put into words it is this: 'Take me; do, please, take me!' 'Take my Lily!' 'No, take me, dear!' Oh, abomination! damnable lie!" And having swallowed the remainder of his tea, he set about removing the cups and vessels.

CHAPTER IX
MERETRICIOUS COSTUMES

"YES," HE RESUMED, putting away his tea and sugar in a bag, "this is the origin of the ascendency of women, from which the entire world is suffering."

"How the ascendency of women?" I asked. "All rights and privileges are on the side of the men."

"Yes, yes; precisely what I was about to say," he interrupted me. "This gives us the clew to the strange circumstance that while, on the one hand, women are reduced to the lowest degree of humiliation, they are all-powerful on the other. Their position in that respect is perfectly analogous to that of the Jews. As these make up for their oppression by acquiring influence and power in other ways, so do women. 'Ah! you ordain,' the Jews seem to say, 'that we should be mere tradesmen? Very well; then we, as tradesmen, shall acquire ascendancy over you.' 'Ah! you ordain that we should be merely instruments of pleasure?' exclaim the women. 'Very well; we shall enslave you.'

"The denial of woman's rights does not consist in her disqualification to vote, to occupy a place upon the bench, to take a part in the conduct of these or those affairs, but in her inferiority to man in all those social acts and functions which are based on the relations of the sexes. Thus it is not in her power to choose her husband, but she must wait to be chosen by him.

[1] [A type of carriage.]

"You say that it would be monstrous to confer upon her these rights? Very well; then let the men be deprived of them. At present they constitute a monopoly for men, and so in order to compensate for the loss of these rights, woman acts upon the senses of the man, and through his senses so completely enslaves him that his right of choice dwindles away to a mere formality. In reality it is she who chooses, and when once she has mastered these means of conquest she abuses them, and acquires thereby a terrible power over men."

"Yes, but in what does this peculiar power manifest itself?" I asked.

"In everything and everywhere," he answered. "Pass by the shops, for instance, in any large city; it is impossible to estimate the untold wealth exhibited in the windows, or to gauge the amount of man's labor which produced it. Observe them well, and in nine tenths of these shops you will find nothing destined for the use of the male members of the community: all the trade in the luxuries of life is called into existence and sustained by the requirements of women. Count up all the factories: by far the greatest number of them turn out useless ornaments, equipages, furniture, toys—for women. Millions of people, generations of slaves, perish in this penal servitude of the factories merely in order to satisfy the whim of woman. Women, like empresses, condemn to imprisonment and hard labor nine tenths of mankind.

"Such is the form assumed by their vengeance on us men for having degraded them and deprived them of equal rights. All these contrivances and stratagems are calculated to act upon the immoral part of our nature and thus to entice us into the nets they have spread for us. Yes, this is the root of the abnormal state of things I have described. Woman has transformed herself into an object of pleasure of such terrible effect that a man can not calmly approach her. No sooner does a man draw near a woman than he falls under the power of her spell, and his senses are forthwith paralyzed. Even in former times I always felt ill at ease in presence of a lady arrayed in all the splendor of ball-dress: at present I positively shudder at the sight, for I recognize therein a palpable danger to people in general, a danger that has no legal right to exist; and I feel prompted to call in a policeman, to appeal for protection against this danger that threatens me, and to insist on its removal or suppression.

"This makes you laugh!" he exclaimed all at once, addressing me; "does it? But this is no joking matter, I can assure you. A time will come, and it may come very soon, when people will realize this, and will ask themselves in wonderment, how it was possible for a society to hold together in which acts like those just described, fraught as they were with danger to the public peace, were tolerated. Can it for a moment be pretended that that bedecking of the human body which our society connives at in women, and which is calculated directly to provoke passion, is devoid of social danger? Positively it is just the same as if you were to set traps and spread nets on the streets and public walks, on the highways and by-ways. Nay, it is still worse. Why is it, let me ask you, that games of hazard are prohibited, while women attired in meretricious costumes are not prohibited? And yet the latter are a thousand times more dangerous than the former!"

CHAPTER X
ONLY A CONDITION

"IT WAS THUS that I, too, was caught. I was what is termed 'in love.' Not only did I represent her to myself as the pink of perfection, but all the time that I was paying my addresses to her I fancied myself also a model of what a man should be. As a matter of fact, the world does not contain a scoundrel of however deep a dye who, if he only made a thorough search, would not discover another scoundrel in some respects worse than himself, and a reason therefore for feeling proud of, and satisfied with, himself.

"That was my case. I did not marry money. Love of lucre played no part in my choice, as it did in that of most of my acquaintances, who married for the sake of their wife's dowry or influential friends. I was wealthy, she was poor. This was one consideration. Another circumstance in which I took equal pride was that others married with the deliberate intention of continuing the irregular lives which they had led before marriage. I, on the contrary, had taken the firm resolution to remain faithful to my wife, after marriage, and there were no bounds to the high opinion I had of myself in consequence. Yes, for this I flattered myself that I was an angel.

"I was only engaged for a short time, and yet I can not recall that period of life without shame. What an abomination! The love that united us was supposed to be of a spiritual character. But if our love and communings had been of a spiritual nature, all the words, phrases, and conversations that passed between us should have expressed this. As a matter of fact, nothing of the kind took place. We found it extremely difficult to converse when left alone; it was a labor of Sisyphus. I would think of something to say, say it, relapse into silence, and then rack my brain for something else—there was absolutely nothing to converse about. All the topics referring to the new life which awaited us, to our future plans, had already been discussed, and what was there further to say? If we had been animals, we should at least have known that we were not expected to converse, but not being mere animals we were forced to speak, notwithstanding that there was absolutely nothing to speak about. Add to all this that disgraceful custom of eating sweets and dinners, and all those abominable preparations for marriage, usual under the circumstances, such as discussions about lodgings, morning robes for my wife, morning coats for myself, linen, toilet, and so on.

"Of course if people contracted marriage in accordance with the rules and counsels of the fathers of the early Russian Church, as the old merchant insisted here this afternoon that they should, down mattresses, the dowry, the bed and bedstead and such-like things would sink to the level of mere details that go along with the sacrament. But in our country, where out of ten who enter into matrimony there is scarcely one who believes, I do not say in the reality of the Sacrament, but in the attribute of the union to create something in the nature of an obligation; where out of one hundred men there is scarcely one who has not been practically married before, or one in fifty who does not propose to commit infidelities whenever a favorable opportunity presents itself; in our country, I say, where the majority look upon the church ceremonies as neither more nor less than a condition, the fulfillment of which entitles them to take possession of a certain woman."

CHAPTER XI
TO BE COMBATED

"THUS IT IS that all people marry; thus it was that I married. Then began the much-lauded period called the honey-moon. What bathos is contained in the very name!

"Strolling about Paris one day," he said, "looking at all the shows and spectacles, I espied a sign-board with the effigy of a woman with a beard and a walrus. I went in to look, and found that the bearded woman was merely a man in a low-bodied woman's dress, and the sea-monster a common dog covered with a walrus's skin swimming about in a bath filled with water. The whole thing was extremely uninteresting. When leaving, the showman deferentially accompanied me, and addressing the public standing outside the door, he pointed at me and said, 'You can ask this gentleman whether the show is worth looking at. Walk in, walk in! One franc a head.' I was ashamed to declare that it was not worth looking at, and the showman undoubtedly relied upon that feeling. It is probably the same with those who have experienced all the fatuities of the honey-moon, and refuse to disabuse others. Nor did I disabuse any one, but I do not see why I should not now tell the truth. Indeed, I feel it incumbent upon me to proclaim the truth about it.

"The fact is it was irksome, miserable, and above all things wearisome, inconceivably wearisome! It reminded me to some extent of the feelings I experienced when I was learning to smoke, years ago, when the nausea in my stomach foreboded sickness, and my mouth was filling with saliva, which I made haste to swallow, endeavoring to look as if the whole thing were pleasant."

"You are speaking curiously of the affairs of a honey-moon," I said. "How are you going to continue the human race if you proceed on the assumption that the fact of two persons living together produces this nausea?"

"Ah! yes; what's to be done, lest the human race perish?" he repeated, maliciously, as if he had been waiting for this conscientious and familiar objection. "Preach abstention from child-bearing, in order that English lords may be always supplied with the wherewithal to wax fat, and no one will find fault with you. But merely hint the advisability of abstaining from child-bearing in the name of morality, and, great heavens! what a cry will be raised!

"But I trust you'll pardon me. That light up there is disagreeable to me," he said, pointing to the lantern; "have you any objection to my drawing the shade round it?" On my replying that it was a matter of indifference to me, he rose—as he did everything—precipitately, got up on the seat, and drew the woolen shade over the lantern.

"Still," I urged, "if every one were to accept this doctrine as a law of practical conduct, the human race would soon cease to exist."

He did not immediately reply.

"You want to know how the human race is to perpetuate itself?" he said, reseating himself opposite to me, stretching out his feet widely apart, and resting his elbows on his knees. "Why should the human race be perpetuated?" he asked.

"Why?" I exclaimed; "because otherwise we should not exist."

"But why should we exist?"

"Why should we? In order to live, of course."

"Well, but why should we live? If there be no purpose, no aim; if life be given to us for life's sake only, then there is no object in living. And if that be so, Schopenhauer and the Buddhists are perfectly right. On the other hand, if there be an end and object in human existence, it is clear that humanity must cease to exist when that object is attained. This is perfectly evident," he repeated with visible emotion, clearly setting a high value upon his thought.

"Yes, this is perfectly evident. Now, mark my words well: if the object for which humanity exists is bliss, goodness, love, or by whatever other name you like to call it, if it is what the ancient prophets have proclaimed it to be, namely, that all men be united in love, that their swords be turned into plowshares, and so on, what hinders the accomplishment of this object? The passions do. Now, of all the passions, the strongest, the most wicked, the most stubborn, is the passion of the senses. Consequently, if we succeed in rooting up the passions, and with them this last and most powerful, the prophecies will come to pass; men will be united by the bond of love, the aim and mission of humanity will have been fulfilled, and there will be no longer any reason for the further existence of the human race.

"As long as humanity subsists, it tends toward an ideal; and its ideal is assuredly not that of rabbits who increase and multiply as much as possible; it is an ideal of goodness attainable by continence, abstemiousness, purity. Toward this ideal people have always been and still are tending.

"Look now at the upshot of all this: love, passion, appears in the role of a safety-valve. The present generation of men has not accomplished the mission for which it is here in the world; and why? Because of its passions, the strongest of which is the passion of sense. On the other hand, such passion not being extirpated, a new generation arises, and humanity has the renewed possibility of arriving at the goal by the efforts of the new men. If they are unsuccessful, it is for the same reason, and failure brings with it the possibility of success later on, and so on ad infinitum, till such times as the object is accomplished, the prophecy comes to pass, and all men are joined together in union.

"What would happen were things otherwise? If God had created men, for instance, for the purpose of accomplishing a certain mission, and had made them mortal and devoid of passions or immortal? In the former case they would live without having attained the end and object of their existence, and would then die; and God would have to resort to another creative act, in order that the purpose in question should be fulfilled. In the latter case, that is, if men had been created immortal, let us suppose that after many thousand years they attained their end—a most unlikely thing to postulate, seeing that it is much easier for new generations to correct the errors of the old and tend toward perfection, than for the same creatures to turn from their mistakes and change their lines of conduct. What would be the aim and purpose of their further existence? What should be done with them then? Evidently things are better as they are.

"But perhaps you dislike the form in which I have expressed all this? Perhaps you are an evolutionist? But even so, you can not fail to see the truth of this contention. The highest race of animals is the human race. In order to hold its own in the struggle with other races it must keep closely together, unite like a swarm of bees, and not go on endlessly multiplying and increasing; and like the bees it should bring up the sexless; that is to say, it ought to aim at restraint, and not by any means contribute to inflame the passions as our social life seems deliberately instituted to do."

He was silent for a time. Then he resumed: "The human race will cease? Yes; but is it possible that any one, no matter from what point of view he contemplated the world, could have ever entertained a doubt about that? Why, it is as inevitable as death. All ecclesiastical doctrines are based on the theory that this world of ours will sooner or later come to an end; modern science propagates the same teaching. Why should we be surprised that ethics inculcates the same lesson?"

Having ceased speaking, he remained a considerable time silent, drinking and smoking the while. Having smoked his cigarette to the end, he took several more out of his bag and began to put them into his old, soiled cigarette-case.

"I understand your position," I said; "something similar to that is taught by the Shakers."

"Yes, yes; and they are right," he exclaimed. "Passion, no matter with what forms it may be hedged round, is an evil, a terrible evil, to be combated, not fostered, as it is in our society. The words of the Gospel that 'whosoever looketh on a woman to lust after her, hath committed adultery with her already in his heart,' apply not only to other men's wives, but also and mainly to one's own. In our world as at present constituted, the prevalent views are exactly contrary to this, and consequently to what they ought to be. What are these wedding tours and excursions, and that isolation of the young married couple authorized by their elders, but a license to unlimited pleasure?"

CHAPTER XII
PUNISHMENT

"BUT SOONER OR later the moral law visits us with condign punishment for every violation of it. Thus all my efforts to make the honey-moon a success were doomed to failure. It was a period of shame, tediousness, and it soon became an unbearable torture.

"Things took this turn very early indeed. Finding my wife bored one day—I think it was the third or fourth day after marriage—I inquired the cause of her gloom, and began to embrace her, this being, to my thinking, all that she could possibly expect or desire from me; but she put my arms off, and began to shed tears. 'What is the matter?' She was unable to say what, but she was evidently very sad and depressed. Probably her nerves revealed to her the nature of our relations; but she could not formulate what she instinctively felt. I continued to question her, and she muttered something about being lonely without her mother. I felt that this was not true, and I set about consoling her without making any reference to her mother. I did not realize that she was simply depressed in spirits, and that her mother was merely a pretext; and yet she at once took offense at my not mentioning her mother, as if I disbelieved what she had told me. She could now see, she said, that I did not love her. On this, I rebuked her for being capricious, and all at once a change came over her face; the sadness that had settled upon it gave way to an expression of irritation, and she began to reproach me in the most spiteful words with being egoistic and cruel. I looked intently upon her; all her features combined to express perfect coldness and hostility—I might almost say hatred—toward me.

"I remember the horror that seized me then; what did it mean? How could it be? Love, the blending of souls in one! And instead of that, this is what it had come to! 'Can it be?' I asked myself. 'Surely this is not she!'

"I endeavored to soothe and calm her, but soon found myself face to face with such an impregnable wall of cold, venomous hostility, that before I knew where I was I was lashed into a state of extreme irritation, with the result that we addressed a number of unpleasant remarks to each other.

"The impression left by that first quarrel of ours was indescribably horrible. I have called it a quarrel, but in truth it was nothing of the kind; it was merely the discovery of the abyss that yawned between us. What we called love had been exhausted, and there we stood face to face in our true mutual relations; two egoists, perfect strangers to each other.

"I have given the name of 'quarrel' to what passed between us. But it was not a quarrel; it was simply a glimpse of our real relation to each other. I did not then perceive that this coldness and hostility constituted our normal relation to each other, because during that first period of our married life those sentiments were soon again hidden from our observation by the vapors raised by 'love,' and I took it that we had merely quarreled and become reconciled, and that no such misunderstandings should ever occur again.

"But it was not long before, during the first month of the honey-moon, another period set in, during which we again ceased for a time to be necessary to each other, and in consequence of which another quarrel broke out. This second misunderstanding impressed me more profoundly than the first. 'The first was not, therefore, a mere accident,' I said to myself; 'it was the result of a necessity, and will again occur in virtue of the same necessity.' Another reason why I was struck more profoundly by this second quarrel, was its absurdly insufficient pretext. It was something about money, which I never grudged, and could not dream of grudging my wife; I only remember that she put such an interpretation upon the matter as to make a remark of mine seem the expression of a wish on my part to acquire an undue ascendency over her by means of money to which she pretended that I claimed an exclusive right. The accusation was groundless, silly, vile, unnatural.

"I lost my temper and upbraided her with lack of delicacy; she accused me in turn, and in the expression of her face and eyes I read the same cruel, deliberate enmity that had struck coldness to my heart before.

"With my father, with my brother, I had quarreled, I remember, occasionally; but there never had subsisted between us that peculiarly bitter hatred that had sprung up between my wife and me. It was not long, however, before this mutual hatred was disguised once more by so-called love, and I was once more engaged in consoling myself that these two quarrels were mistakes, mere misunderstandings which might be easily cleared up. The occurrence of the third and fourth quarrels, however, dispelled this delusion; I recognized clearly that this was no accident, no misunderstanding, but the outcome of necessity; that it could not be otherwise, that it would recur again and again.

"And my heart froze within me at the perspective before me. My suffering was still further intensified by the thought that I alone was living with my wife in such perpetual discord, so different from the way I used to flatter myself we would live; that other people were more fortunate than we were. I was ignorant then that this is the common lot, that other people believe their misery to be—as I believed mine—exceptional; that they not only hide it from others, but endeavor to disguise it to themselves.

"In our case it began immediately after the wedding, and went on gaining gradually in intensity and savageness. From the very first weeks of our married life I knew in the bottom of my heart that I was caught in a trap, that what I had realized was not what I had had in view and confidently expected, that my marriage, far from being a source of happiness, was a burden very hard to bear: but, like every one else, I refused to admit this, not only to others—I should not own to it now if it were not ended forever—but even to myself.

"Whenever I think of it now, it is a mystery to me how I could have remained blind to my real condition. One sure sign by which we might have easily recognized it was the circumstance that all our quarrels turned upon mere bagatelles; indeed, their origin was so absurdly trivial that, once over, we could not recollect how they had come about. The reasoning faculty was not quick enough to conjure up specious pretexts fast enough for the outburst of cordial hostility which continued to subsist between us without break or change. Still more striking, however, was the insufficiency of the pretexts for reconciliation. Occasionally they assumed the form of words, explanations, even tears, but at times—and even now the recollection of it fills me with disgust—while launching the most bitter and venomous reproaches at each other, a period of silence would begin, filled up with smiles, kisses, embraces."

CHAPTER XIII

TWO WAYS OUT

AT THIS POINT two passengers entered the carriage and began to install themselves on the far-off seat. Pozdnischeff ceased speaking till they had finally taken their places. As soon as they were settled down, and the noise caused by their movements had subsided, he began again where he had left off, obviously never for a moment losing the thread of his thoughts.

"What is peculiarly revolting about all this," he resumed, "is that whereas in theory love is described as an ideal state, a sublime sentiment, in practice it is a thing which can not be mentioned or called to mind without a feeling of disgust. It was not without cause that nature made it so. But if it be revolting, let it be proclaimed so without any disguise. Instead of that, however, people go about preaching and teaching that it is something splendid and sublime.

" 'What,' I asked myself in astonishment, 'could give rise to the deadly malignity which we entertained toward each other?' And yet the source of it was perfectly obvious. This malignity was neither more nor less than the protest of human nature against the other nature that was crushing it in both of us. I was amazed at our reciprocal hatred. And yet it was impossible that we should feel anything but hatred for each other. This sentiment was, in kind, identical with the hatred which accomplices in a crime feel for each other, both for instigating and for actually taking part in the crime.

"Perhaps you think that I am wandering from the point? Not in the least. I am unfolding to you the story of how I killed my wife. They asked me on my trial with what and how I killed her. Fools that they are, to suppose that I murdered her with the knife on the 5th of October. It was not then that I killed her; it was very long before, just as they are all killing their wives at this moment—all, ay, all of them."

"How so?" I asked.

"It is the most extraordinary thing conceivable that no one wants to see what is so clear and evident, what physicians should know and inculcate, but about which they are obstinately silent.

"The thing is so extremely simple. Now the number of women in the world is about equal to that of men. The inference is clear: it is drawn and acted upon by the lower animals, and it requires no rare wisdom on the part of men to discover it; it is that restraint is indispensable. But simple as is the discovery, it has not yet been made. Science has discovered some new kind of animalcula that swim about in the blood, and a hundred other superfluous absurdities, but it has not advanced to the point necessary to apprehend this truth yet. At least one does not hear of any such doctrines being put forward by men of science.

"And so a woman has but two ways out of the difficulty. The first is by annihilating once for all or destroying, whenever the circumstances seem to require it, her faculty of becoming a mother. The second is not, properly speaking, a way out of the difficulty at all; it is simply a direct violation of the laws of nature: the woman is obliged to nurse her child and be the mistress of her husband at one and the same time. This is the origin in our social sphere of hysterics and nerves, and in the peasant class of 'possession.' So it is in Russia. Nor is it otherwise in Europe. And both women suffering from 'possession' and the female patients of Professor Charcot[1] are in the true sense of the word cripples; and of such the world is full.

"It needs but little reflection to realize how important, how sublime, is that which is taking place when a woman bears within her, or is tending and feeding, the being that will prove a continuation of, a substitute for, ourselves. And these holy functions are interrupted, and for what? . . . And in the face of this they prate about freedom, about woman's rights. Why, the cannibals might just as well boast that they were solicitous for the rights and liberty of the prisoners of war whom they feed and fatten for food."

[1] [Pioneer psychiatrist.]

All this was new to me, and deeply impressed me.

"What would you do?" I asked. "If you are right you will annihilate the relation of husband and wife; and men, as you are aware—"

"Yes, I know," he interrupted. "This is another of the favorite doctrines of physicians, those precious priests of science. I would, if I could, condemn these magicians to discharge the functions of these very women whom they affirm to be so indispensable to men, in order to hear what they then would say upon the question. Impress a man with the idea that alcohol is indispensable to him, that he can not get on without tobacco, that opium is a necessity of life, and all these things will straightway become indispensable. Is it to be supposed that God did not know what was needful to man, and that not having taken counsel of the physicians He scamped His work?

"It was a question, as you perceive, of reconciling two conditions diametrically opposed to each other. How was the difficulty to be overcome? Put your trust in the doctors; they will make things smooth. And they did. They found an issue out of the difficulty. Oh, that those villains were divorced from their frauds! It is indeed high time! You see what it has come to already. People go mad and blow their brains out, and all owing to this. And how could it be otherwise?

"Brute beasts seem to be instinctively aware that their progeny serves to perpetuate the race, and they observe a certain law in this connection. Man alone does not know this, and does not want to know it. He wrecks and ruins one half of the human race; he transforms all women, who should be active coadjutors aiding humanity to move onward toward truth and happiness, into enemies of progress and development. Look around you and say what or who it is that impedes the advance of humanity. Womankind. And why do they act so? For the reason just explained.

"Yes, yes," he repeated several times, beginning to stir himself a little, and he took out a cigarette and began to smoke it, obviously striving to calm himself.

CHAPTER XIV

THE DEVIL'S CUNNING

"I LIVED THIS life like everybody else, and, what was still worse, I flattered myself that because I did not commit adultery I was leading a pure family life, was a truly moral man, perfectly blameless, and that if quarrels did disturb the quiet of our lives my wife was in fault, it was her character that was to blame. Needless to say the blame did not really rest with her. She was like other women, like the majority of women. She had been brought up in such a way as to qualify her to play the part assigned to women in our society, which is equivalent to saying that her training was in nowise different from that of other women of the well-to-do classes.

"It is the fashion nowadays to talk about some new system of female education, but all that is arrant nonsense. Women are actually trained and educated in perfect harmony with the views really and truly held in modern society respecting the mission of their sex, and female education will always be regulated in strict accordance with man's conception of woman. Now no one ignores what men's views of women are. Wine, women, and song—so say the poets in verse. Read the poetry of all ages and countries, examine all the productions of painting and sculpture, commencing with erotic poems and Venuses and Phrynes,[1] and you can not fail to perceive that in the highest society, as well as in the lowest, woman is merely an instrument of pleasure.

"And mark the devil's cunning; it is not enough that she should be so degraded, but the fact must be deftly disguised. Thus in by-gone times we read of the gallant knights who went about protesting that they idolized woman, apotheosized her; in our days men profess that they honor and respect woman; they yield up their places to her, pick up her pocket-handkerchief, and some even go so far as to admit her right to occupy all civil positions of trust, to have a share in the government, and so on. And in the face of all these professions and protestations the world's view of woman's mission and position is unmodified; she is still what she was—an object of pleasure; and she is well aware that it is so.

"We notice exactly the same state of things, the same contradiction between professions and acts in the matter of slavery. Slavery is the enjoyment by a few of the involuntary labor of the many, and before slavery can become a thing of the past, people must cease to desire the enjoyment of the forced labor of others, must hold it to be sinful or shameful. But no, they simply set to work to abolish the outward form of slavery, to render it impossible legally to purchase or sell a slave, and execute a deed of sale; and this done, they delude themselves into the belief that slavery no longer exists, overlooking the circumstance that it continues to be just as rife as before, because people still consider it good and just to profit by the labor of others. And as long as they hold it to be good and just there will never be any lack of persons stronger or more cunning than their fellows who can transform this opinion into an act.

[1] [Courtesans; Phryne was a famous ancient Greek courtesan.]

"It is just the same with the thralldom of woman. Woman's serfdom consists in the circumstance that she is looked upon and sought after as an instrument of pleasure, and that this view is considered the right one. And then woman is solemnly enfranchised, is invested with extensive rights, equal to those exercised by men, but people continue to regard her as an instrument of pleasure, continue to educate her accordingly, instilling those views into her mind first in her childhood, and later on by means of public opinion. And so she remains what she was, a degraded, demoralized serf, as the man remains what he was, a demoralized slave-owner. We enfranchise woman in high schools and hospital wards, and yet continue to look upon her as before. Train her, as she is trained in Russia, to regard herself in that light, and she will remain forever a being of a lower order. Gymnasiums and high schools are powerless to change this; it can only be altered by a change in men's views of women and women's views of themselves. It can only be supplanted by a better state of things when woman considers that the highest condition to which she, as woman, can attain is that of maidenhood—a state which she now regards as one of shame and disgrace. Until this change of ideas takes place, the ideal of every girl, whatever her education may be, will necessarily remain what it now is—to attract as many men as possible, in order to secure for herself the possibility of choosing; and the circumstance that one girl knows more mathematics, or another can play the harp, does not change one iota. A woman is happy, and attains all that she desires, when she captivates a man; hence the great object of her life is to master the art of captivating men. So it has ever been, and so it will be. In the life of a young girl in our sphere this tendency is clearly observable, and she carries it with her into the married state. To the maiden it is indispensable in order that she may have an extensive choice; to the married woman that she may strengthen her ascendency over her husband. The only event that puts an end to this tendency, or at least represses it for awhile, is the birth of children, and even that has no effect if the mother is a monster—that is, does not nurse her own children. But here again the doctors interfere.

"My wife, who suckled her five other children, fell ill soon after the birth of the first. The precious doctors who cynically touched and examined her, for which I had to thank and pay them, decreed that she should not suckle her child, and, in consequence of this sentence, she was deprived of the sole means whereby she would have been effectually delivered from coquettishness. We hired a wet-nurse—that is to say, we took advantage of the poverty, the misery, and the ignorance of another woman, enticed her away from her own child to ours, and in return decked her out with a head-dress and tawdry laces. But this by the way.

The point is that my wife's exemption from the cares and duties of a mother manifested itself in the awakening of that female coquettishness which had previously lain dormant in her, while I began to be tortured with the agonies of jealousy, which had never given me a moment's rest during my married life, but now grew unbearably excruciating. This feeling of jealousy is no peculiar characteristic of mine; it is the common lot of all husbands who live with their wives as I lived with mine."

CHAPTER XV
PANGS OF JEALOUSY

"DURING THE WHOLE course of my married life I never once enjoyed a moment's relief from the maddening pangs of jealousy. There were times, however, when my torments were unusually acute; and one of these periods began after the birth of my first child when the doctors forbid my wife to nurse it.

"There was a twofold reason for this intensity of jealousy during the period in question. In the first place, the circumstance that my wife experienced that uneasiness peculiar to mothers which provokes a general disturbance in the natural course of life; and secondly, because, having seen with what a light heart she set at naught the moral obligations of a mother, I naturally, if unconsciously, concluded that she might with equal facility trample upon the duties of wife, especially as she was in the enjoyment of perfect health, and, in spite of the prohibition of the precious physicians, nursed the children who were born subsequently without the slightest inconvenience to herself."

"You do not seem enamored of doctors?" I said, noticing an especially bitter tone of voice whenever he alluded to them or their profession.

"It's not a matter of like or dislike," he answered. "My life has been utterly wrecked by doctors, and they have ruined and are still ruining the lives of thousands, nay, of hundreds of thousands, and I can not well help putting cause and effect together. Of course it is natural enough that, like lawyers and members of other professions, they should be somewhat keen about earning money, and I must say that I would most willingly cede them half my yearly income, and I am sure every one else would gladly follow my example, if their influence for evil were made clear, on condition that they would refrain from meddling in other people's family affairs, that they would keep to themselves and leave others in peace. Although I never collected statistics on the subject, I am acquainted with scores of cases—and there are countless similar ones—in which they killed now the unborn child, now the mother, on the pretext of performing an operation. Yet nobody ever regards these murders, as no one ever added up the murders committed by the Inquisition, because, forsooth, they are all done for the good of mankind. It would be impossible to count the number of crimes committed by the medical profession. And yet they are all as dust in the balance, compared with that moral depravation, the pollution of materialism, which they introduce into the world through the medium of women. If you hearken to their counsels—so numerous and dangerous are the germs of disease that lurk in wait for you at every step you take—whatever you do will tend not to draw you closer to your fellowmen, but to separate you from them more than ever. If the doctors' behests were faithfully carried out, every one of us should sit apart, completely isolated from every one else, and would never think of putting the syringe with the carbolic acid out of his hand. (Of late, I am told, they have discovered that carbolic acid is ineffectual.) This, however, is merely by the way. The real poison of their influence lies in the demoralization of the people, especially of the women, which marks their track. Nowadays it would be a solecism to say: 'You, friend, are leading a bad, irregular life; live better.' No one would ever think of addressing such words to himself or to others. If you are leading a bad life, the cause is to be sought for in the nervous centers, in one of which something must have gone wrong; and you can not do better than put yourself in the hands of a physician who will prescribe a shilling's worth of medicine for you, which you will duly take as ordered. You will then grow worse, on which you must have more doctors and more medicines. A precious system!

"But all this by the way. I wanted to say that my wife nursed the children herself with excellent results, and that this child-bearing and child-nursing were the only things that contributed to ease the sufferings I endured from jealousy. Indeed, had it not been for them, the catastrophe would have occurred much sooner. It was the children who saved both her and me. In the course of eight years she gave birth to five children and nursed them all herself."

"Where are they now—your children, I mean?" I asked.

"The children?" he repeated, with a frightened look.

"I beg your pardon; perhaps I have unwittingly awakened very painful memories."

"No, it's nothing. My sister-in-law and her brother took charge of the children. I gave them my fortune, but they refused to give me the custody of my children. You see I am a sort of insane person. I am now journeying away from them. I saw them, but they would not give them up to me. If I had charge of them, I should educate them so that they would not resemble their parents; and this is precisely what is not wanted. It is required that they should be exactly such as we were. Well, there is no help for it, I dare say. It is natural enough for them to keep the children from me and to disbelieve me. Besides, I am not at all sure that I have the energy needed to educate them; indeed, I am inclined to think not: I am but a ruin now, a cripple. One thing, however, I have; I know—yes, *this* is true, I do know what most other people will not soon learn. Yes, the children are all living, and growing up just such savages as all those around them. I saw them. Three times I saw them. I can do nothing for them. Nothing. I am now on my way to my place in the south, where I have a little house and garden. Yes, it will take some time before people will know what I know. It is easy to learn whether there is much iron in the sun, and what other metals there are in the sun and the stars; but it is hard, yes, frightfully hard, to discover that which convicts us of immorality. You are listening, and even for that I am grateful."

CHAPTER XVI
A BLESSING AND JOY

"YOU JUST MENTIONED the children. There again, just consider what lying goes on concerning children. Children are a blessing from God, children are a joy. Now all this is a lie. It was true once, but has long since ceased to contain a grain of truth. Children are a torment, and nothing more. The majority of mothers distinctly feel this, and at times, when off their guard, say so very plainly. Question the general run of mothers in our social circles, people who live in affluence and they will tell you that from fear lest their children should sicken and die, they don't wish to have any children at all; and if any are born, they refuse to nurse them, lest they should become too much attached to them and be made unhappy in consequence. The pleasure they receive from the contemplation of the child, the charms of its tiny hands, its pretty little feet, and its diminutive little body, are less than the sufferings they undergo in consequence of—I do not say the illness or loss of the child, but of—the mere apprehension of the possibility of illness or death. Having weighed the advantages and the drawbacks, it turns out that the balance is not in favor of the former, and they therefore decide that it is not desirable to have children. These sentiments they express artlessly, fearlessly, thinking that they spring from affection for children—an excellent, praiseworthy feeling in which they take pride. They do not perceive that by reasoning in this way, they are disavowing love, and merely proclaiming their own selfishness. Their pleasure is lessened by fear for the child, and consequently they do not wish to have a child whom they would be fond of. They sacrifice, not themselves for a beloved creature, but the beloved creature who is on the point of coming into existence for themselves. It is pretty clear that this is not love but egoism.

"On the other hand, one has not the heart to condemn these mothers of well-to-do families for their egoism, when one bears in mind all that they have to suffer for the sake of their children's health, owing once more to those doctors who play such an important part in our lives. Even now the bare recollection of what my wife went through, and the continual state of anxiety she was in during the first years of our married life, when we had three and four children who engrossed all her attention, makes me shudder. We led a dog's life. It does not deserve the name of life; it was one never-ending danger hanging over us, followed by momentary escapes from it, after which it would again loom threatening until we once more escaped for a time, and so on without end—our condition being for all the world like that of the crew of a sinking vessel. There were times when I imagined that all this was feigned, and that she was merely pretending to be anxious about the children in order to get the whip hand of me, so effectually did it contribute to settle all questions between us in her favor. It seemed as if everything she said and did was said and done as the result of a preconcerted plan. This, however, was not really so. She was continually worrying and tormenting herself to death with the children, with their health and their illnesses, and it was a martyrdom for her as well as for me. She felt that strong attachment to children, that animal need of nursing, fondling, and nestling them which is common to most mothers. But she did not enjoy, as animals do, immunity from imagination and reasoning. The hen, for instance, has no fear of what may be in store for her chick, has not the faintest notion what the diseases are to which it may fall a prey; knows nothing of the means by which people fondly imagine that they can save themselves from sickness and death; and consequently her young are not a torment to her. She does for her chicks what it is in her nature to do for them, and what is therefore a pleasure for her to do, and it is only natural that her young should be a joy to her. And the instant one of her chicks falls ill, her duties become very clearly determined: she has only to warm and feed it, and having done this feels that she has performed all that is needful. If it comes to pass, in spite of her care, that it dies, she does not ask why and whither it has gone; she clucks for awhile, ceases, and lives on as before.

"With our unhappy women, and with my wife in particular, the case is very different. Independently of the question of children's diseases and the way to treat them, there were numbers of other topics always cropping up, such, for instance, as how to educate them, how to discipline their minds, about which she had heard and read an infinite number of every-varying rules and prescriptions. They should be fed thus, and only with that and that; no, not so, not with that, but thus and with such and such a food. On the subjects of clothing them, bathing them, putting them to sleep, sending them to walk, regulating the quality of the air they breathe, both of us were discovering, but especially she was discovering, new rules every week. It was just as if children had only begun to be born into the world yesterday. It was all because the poor child was not fed properly, or did not get its bath in due time, that it fell ill; consequently she felt that it was she who should bear the blame, for not having taken the needful precautions, for not having done what should have been done.

"Thus under the most favorable circumstances, that is, when in thriving health, children are a torment; but when they fall ill, life is positively not worth living, it is simply a hell on earth. We start with the postulate that diseases can be cured, that there is a science which has their treatment for its object, and that there are people called physicians who know how to cure them. Not, of course, that every doctor is capable of treating them successfully, but the best among the profession. And now, the child being ill, the problem to be solved is how to get at the very best doctor, the man who saves; this done, the infant is saved. If you can not consult him, if you are living in a different part of the city from where he resides, and can not summon him in time, the child is lost. And observe, it is not the belief of my wife only to which I am now giving expression, it is the faith of all the women of her social sphere. On all sides scraps of conversation like the following fell frequently on her ears: 'Mrs. A——'s three children, poor dear things, died because Doctor Z—— was not sent for in time. He saved Mrs. D——'s eldest little girl, you know. The Petroffs, by advice of the doctor, isolated themselves in time and went to live at different hotels, and saved their lives by doing so. The others who did not isolate themselves lost their children. Mrs. So-and-So's little girl was very weak until, by advice of the doctor, they went to live in the south, and saved the child's life.' How could she do otherwise than fret, and chafe, and tremble, from year's end to year's end, at the thought that the life of her children, to whom she was attached by the bonds of strong animal affection, depended wholly on her learning in good time what Doctor Ivan Zakharievitch had to say on the subject. And yet nobody knew what Ivan Zakharievitch would say, he himself least of all, because he was and is well aware that he knows nothing and has no help to give, and so all he does is to shuffle and trim as best he can, so that people should not cease to believe that he knows what he is talking about.

"If she had been in all respects an animal, she would not have tortured herself as she did. If she had been in all respects a human being, she would have been animated by faith in God, and would have spoken, and thought like the peasant women, who exclaim: 'God gave and God has taken away; you can not escape from God.' She would have felt that the life and death of all mankind, and of her children among the rest, are beyond the power of man, in the hands of God alone, and she would not therefore have racked her mind with the thought that it was in her power to hinder the sickness and death of her children, and that yet she failed to do so. As a matter of fact, her position was extremely complicated: she had charge of the most frail creatures conceivable, weak little things exposed to countless mishaps. She was drawn toward them by vehement animal affection. Moreover, these beings were confided to her care, and yet the means of preserving them unharmed were hidden from her and revealed to men who were perfect strangers to her, whose services and counsels she could not obtain otherwise than by paying considerable sums of money, and not always even then. How could she do otherwise than torture herself?

"And this she did without respite. Just when our angry passions would be slowly subsiding after some scene of jealousy or a common quarrel, and we were making ready to regulate our lives anew, to begin a course of reading or to take some enterprise in hand, word would be suddenly brought that Vasa was taken sick; that Mary had a bowel complaint; that a rash had broken out on Andy's face or body, and from that moment began our martyrdom anew. To what part of the city should we rush off, which doctor should we send for, in what room should we isolate the sick child? And then began the endless series of injections, measurings of temperature, mixtures, potions, and doctors. And before this came to an end, something else would crop up unexpectedly, and so on without end; a regular, family life being wholly out of the question. As I said before, it was one continual escape from fancied and from real dangers. And the same thing goes on still in the majority of families. In our family it was painfully palpable. My wife loved her children dearly, and was credulous; so that the presence of children, far from contributing to better our life, only poisoned it.

"Moreover, the children were for us a new pretext for quarreling. Each of us specially favored one child, which was our pet instrument in the quarrel. Thus, I generally employed Vasa (the eldest); she made use of Liza. Later on, when they grew up and their characters unfolded themselves, they gradually became our allies, whom we sought to enlist on our side by every means at our disposal. The results told terribly on their bringing up, poor things; but we had no time or desire during our endless warfare to give this a thought. The girl was usually my partisan; the eldest boy, who resembled his mother, and frequently espoused her cause, was often hateful to me."

CHAPTER XVII
HOSTILE

"AND IN THIS manner we continued to live, our relations growing gradually more and more hostile, until at last it was no longer difference of views that produced enmity, but settled enmity that engendered difference of views. No matter what opinion she might advance, no matter what wish she might express, I always dissented in advance, and she treated me in the same way. In the fourth year of our marriage we tacitly came to the conclusion that there was no hope of our ever being able to understand each other, to agree with each other, and so we ceased to make any further attempts to come to an agreement. Each of us held his or her own opinion about the most matter-of-fact subjects—about everything connected with the children, for instance. The views that I advocated were not by any means so dear to me that I could not sacrifice them; but she was of the opposite way of thinking; and to give up my opinion would mean to yield to her; and, whatever else I might agree to, this I could not think of doing. It was the same with her. She looked upon herself as having acted rightly and justly by me, and I, in my own eyes, was invariably immaculate. When together, we were reduced to something like silence, to such conversations as the very brutes, I am convinced, can carry on among themselves. 'What o'clock is it?' 'Is it time to go to bed?' 'What shall we have for dinner to-day?' 'Where shall we drive?' 'What's in the newspapers?' 'Shall I send for the doctor? Mary has a sore throat.'

"A single step beyond the bounds of this circumscribed circle of conversational topics was enough to provoke the renewal of hostilities. Skirmishes and expressions of hatred were called forth by the coffee, the table-cloth, the carriage, the card played at whist—in a word, by things and incidents that could not possibly be of the slightest importance to us. Speaking for myself, I can say that I was boiling with hatred toward her. I would watch her pouring out the tea, waving her foot to and fro, lifting up the spoon to her mouth, smacking her lips and drawing in the liquid; and I hated her for all that as if she had committed a really bad action. I did not remark at the time that these periods of hatred recurred regularly, uniformly, and invariably corresponded with the periods of what we termed love.

"The periods and the degrees corresponded: after a period of love came a period of hatred; a period of vehement love was followed by a long period of hatred; a shorter period of hatred succeeded a weaker manifestation of love. We were not then aware that this love and hatred were the two opposite poles of one and the same feeling.

"It would have been terrible to live thus, had we realized and understood our position; but we did not understand it. And herein lies the salvation, as well as the punishment, of men who lead irregular lives; that they can always raise a cloud before their eyes which hides from them the misery of their situation. It was thus that we acted. She sought to forget the dreadful reality by giving her attention to absorbing and always urgent occupations: household cares, the furniture, her own dresses and those of the children, their schooling, and their health. As for me, I had my own ways of intoxicating myself. There was the intoxication of my daily work, the intoxication of the chase, the intoxication of cards. Thus we were both of us always occupied; and both of us felt that the more assiduously we were occupied, the more spiteful and malicious we could be to each other.

" 'It's all right for you to go on making your grimaces,' I would say of her to myself; 'but you worried me to death all last night with those scenes you made; and here now I've got to go to the meeting of the committee.' 'You have no reason to feel uneasy,' she on her side would not only think, but say aloud to me, 'but I have not slept a wink all night with the child.'

"All these new-fangled theories about hypnotism, psychical disorders, hysterics, and the rest, are an absurdity, not a simple absurdity, however, but a wicked, baneful absurdity. There is not the slightest doubt that Charcot would have pronounced my wife to be hysterical and myself abnormal, and it is likely enough that he would set about treating us. And yet there was absolutely nothing to cure us of.

"And thus we lived in a perpetual fog, unable to see and realize the position in which we were. And if the episode which occurred later on had not taken place at all, I might live to be an old man without once ceasing to cherish the belief that I had led a good life; not a remarkably good one, but not a bad life. I might never have got a glimpse of that abyss of misery and odious lying in which I was floundering hopelessly. We were two prisoners hating each other and chained together. We poisoned each other's lives, and tried to shut our eyes to what we were doing. I did not know at that time that ninety-nine per cent of all married people are plunged in just such a hell as mine. I was not aware then that I was in such a hell, and consequently never imagined that others were.

"It is wonderful what striking coincidences may be found in the course of a regular humdrum life, and even in quite an irregular life. Thus, just when the parents have rendered each other's life unbearable, it becomes necessary, in the interests of their children's education, to come to live in a city where the conditions for education are favorable." He was silent for awhile. Then he uttered those peculiar sounds, which now resembled suppressed sobs. We were nearing a station. "What o'clock is it?" he asked me. I looked at my watch—it was two o'clock, A.M. "Are you not tired?" he exclaimed. "No, I am not, but you are fatigued," I replied. "I am choking," he said; "excuse me, I will get out for awhile at the station and take a drink of water;" and reeling down the passage in the middle of the carriage, he left the train. I remained seated alone in the compartment, turning over in my mind all that he had been telling me, and so absorbed was I by my reflections that I did not remark his return by the opposite door.

CHAPTER XVIII
NO CURB

"I KNOW I am continually wandering away from the subject, but the fact is I have pondered long and carefully over it all, and I have come to look upon many things from a new angle of vision, and I would rather explain all this to you in detail.

"As I was saying, we left the country and came to settle in the city. In a city unhappy people breathe much more freely than in the country. A man may live a hundred years in a city without the fact ever once dawning upon him that he has been dead and rotten for ever so long. He has no leisure to take stock of himself; he is always occupied; there are social rounds and duties, the arts, his own and his children's health to look after, their education to superintend; he must receive the visits of these people and of those, must in turn visit these acquaintances and those friends, must see this person and hear that one. A city, no matter when you consider it, is never without one or more celebrities, of whose presence it is absolutely incumbent upon you to avail yourself; now you must have yourself treated for this or that complaint, or have your children prescribed for; then again you have to see the teacher, the tutor, the governess—and your life is a hollow sham.

"It was thus that we lived, growing less susceptible to the sufferings caused by our daily intercourse. Moreover, at first we had the pleasing pastime of settling down in the city, establishing ourselves in our new lodgings, and the consequent journeying to and fro between the city and the country.

"The second winter after our arrival an incident occurred without which none of the subsequent episodes of my life would ever have taken place. She was delicate in health, and the scoundrelly doctors forbid her ever again to become a mother. And they taught her the means of executing their commands. To me this was an abomination, and I set my face against it; but she insisted on obeying the doctors, stubbornly refusing to yield to my representations. To the peasant workman children are necessary, although he finds it hard enough to support them; but they are necessary, and this is the justification of his conjugal relations. To us who possess children already, they are not a necessity; on the contrary, they are a source of new anxiety, of expense—they are a burden, in a word. Consequently we are without any justification of the life we lead. Either we escape from having children by artificial means, or else—what is still worse—we regard them as a misfortune, the result of carelessness on our part. But justification we have already absolutely none. So low are we fallen, however, from a moral point of view, that we do not feel the need of any justification. The overwhelming majority of the present educated classes give themselves up to this species of life without the least remorse of conscience. Nor would it be easy to expect remorse, seeing that there is no such thing as conscience in our life, unless we consent to give that name to the conscience of public opinion, of the criminal law. And in the present case neither of the two is shocked or in any way called into play. There is no reason why one should be ashamed to look society in the face, for all its members do likewise, Mrs. P——, and Ivan Zakharievitch, and the rest. Neither need one be in awe of the criminal law. It is only ugly country girls and soldiers' wives who throw their children into wells and ponds: and it is of course only just that such depraved characters as they are should be put in jail. We arranged all these things in good time, decently, respectably.

"Two years more rolled by, and it became evident that the means supplied by the doctors were beginning to act. My wife's appearance improved; she grew more attractive than ever with the last mellow beauty, as it were, of summer. She felt this, and thought much about herself. Her beauty was of a provoking, perturbing kind, such as would naturally characterize a pretty woman of thirty, well-fed, irritable, and no longer fatigued by the cares and responsibilities of motherhood. Whenever she passed she was sure to attract the looks of men, to magnetize them, as it were. She resembled a well-fed, wanton, harnessed horse that has long stood inactive in the stables, and from whom the bridle has been suddenly removed. There was no curb of any kind, as there is no curb of any kind to hold in ninety-nine per cent of our women. I felt this, and I was seized with horror."

CHAPTER XIX
THE VIOLINIST

HE SUDDENLY ROSE and moved nearer to the window. "I ask your pardon," he said, and silently fixing his eyes on the window, remained thus three or four minutes. Then, heaving a deep sigh, he again rose and reseated himself opposite me.

His face underwent a total change; there was a piteous expression in his eyes, and a strange kind of smile played about his lips. "I am a little tired. But I will go on with my story. There's still plenty of time, the day has not dawned yet."

"Yes," he began, after having lighted a cigarette, "she throve and grew stouter from the time when she ceased to bear children, and her malady—the endless worry and anxiety about the children—began to disappear. It seemed as if she were recovering.

"Yes, she seemed to have recovered her senses as after a drunken fit, to have awakened to the fact that there was a whole God's world full of joys and happiness which she had somehow forgotten, in which she had not known how to live. 'I must endeavor not to let this slip away from my grasp; time will fly by very quickly, and it will be too late.' This at least is what I fancied she thought, or, rather, felt; and I do not see how she could have thought or felt otherwise, seeing that all her education had had but the one object of persuading her that there is only one thing worthy of attention in the world, that thing being so-called 'love.' She had married, and had experienced something of that 'love,' but not by any means as much as she had expected, not that which she had promised herself, and which she longed for. Moreover, she had met with many disappointments, disillusions, sufferings in marriage, among them the torture of which she had never even dreamed—children. This species of suffering had wearied and harassed her until the obliging doctors came along and informed her how to shirk the duties of motherhood. So she rejoiced, tried the doctors' method, and revived; living and breathing for one sole purpose—'love.'

"But love with a husband whom jealousy and hate rendered odious was not what she yearned for, and she began to dream of another love, pure and new—at least, I thought so—looking about her in vague expectation, as it were, of something. I saw this, and could not but feel uneasy in consequence, especially as about this time she would lose no opportunity of expressing such thoughts in conversation with others, intending them, of course, for my ear; and this notwithstanding the fact that only an hour previously she might have said just the opposite. Thus she would often maintain, half seriously, half in jest, that maternal solicitude is a delusion; that it is a pity to sacrifice one's youth for one's children instead of taking one's share of the joys of living. She cared less for her children then, and more for herself, attending to her personal appearance—though she tried to conceal this—to her pleasures, and even seeking to perfect herself in certain accomplishments. Thus she set herself again to practice music—she had formerly played the piano with a certain technical skill and delicacy—and this was the visible beginning of the catastrophe." He again turned toward the window, and looked out with wearied eyes; but making a visible effort to control himself, he continued. "Yes, it was then that that individual appeared on the scene." He faltered, and twice made the peculiar noise that characterized him. I could see that it was extremely painful to him to name that man, to mention or in any way allude to him. But he made an effort, and having, as it were, broken through the barrier that held him back, he went on with determination—"A vile fellow he was in my eyes. This I say, not because of the important part he played in my life, but because it is really so. But the fact that he was a sorry character only shows what an irresponsible being she was. Had it not been this man it would have been another. It was necessary that this thing should come to pass." He was again silent for a moment. "He was a musician, a violinist, partly a professional, partly a fashionable amateur. His father, a land-owner, had been my father's neighbor, and had ruined himself financially years ago. He had three children, all boys, who were provided for in one way or another; the youngest being sent to his god-mother in Paris, where he had studied in the Academy of Music, as he had a gift for music, and he came out a violinist and took part in public concerts. He was a man who—"

Wishing to say something bitter Pozdnischeff made an evident effort to restrain himself, and, speaking very rapidly, continued:

"I don't know how he lived then, I only know that he came back to Russia that year and called upon me. He had almond-shaped humid eyes, rosy smiling lips, waxed mustaches, his hair was cut and dressed in the latest fashion, his face was of the insipidly agreeable kind which women term 'not bad-looking,' he was of weak build, but not misshapen. He was inclined to strike up a tone of familiarity to the full extent, which the circumstances seemed to justify, but he was at the same time peculiarly sensitive, and always prepared to stop short if he met with the slightest check or discouragement—not, however, without a due regard for his own outward dignity. His boots, of the approved Parisian shade, were with buttons, his necktie always of some crying color—in a word, he had adopted all those little peculiarities which take the attention of all foreigners in Paris, and by their originality and novelty catch the eye of a woman and prepossess her in favor of the wearer. Outwardly he was always good-humored. He had a way of speaking about everything by means of allusions and fragmentary expressions, just as if you knew all about it and remembered it vividly, and could finish his phrases for him. This was the man who with his music was the cause of all that followed.

"On my trial all the facts of the case were dove-tailed together in such a manner as to make it appear as if I had killed my wife from jealousy. This was not so; at least, I mean it requires to be considerably modified before it can be said to be true. No doubt was entertained in court that my wife had sinned against me, and that I had killed her to avenge my outraged honor—that is what they call it—and I was acquitted in consequence. I endeavored on my trial to put the facts in their true light, but my efforts were interpreted as the result of a desire on my part to rehabilitate my wife's good name. But in truth her relations to that musician, whatever they may have been, mattered really very little to me or to her either. What did matter very much is what I have already related to you. It was all caused by the fact that there was that yawning bottomless abyss between her and me because of the terrible strain of mutual hatred whereby the slightest touch, the least impulsion, was quite sufficient to precipitate the crisis. Quarrels, too, had grown very frequent between us at that time, and were unusually savage; alternating, as of old, with outbursts of headstrong animal appetites. If he had not come upon the scene some one else would have played his part as effectually. If one pretext of jealousy had not been forthcoming another would have been unearthed. What I mean to affirm is that all husbands who live as I live must sooner or later give themselves up to indulgence or separate from their wives, or else must kill themselves or their wives as I killed mine. If there are people to whom none of these alternatives has proved a necessity, they are very rare exceptions. Before I ended as I did I was several times on the point of committing suicide, and more than once my wife had attempted to poison herself."

CHAPTER XX
LIAR! LIAR!

"SOMETHING OF THE kind had taken place a short time before the catastrophe. We had been living for a little while, during a cessation of hostilities, a kind of informal truce, and in the absence of grounds for violating it we began to talk about a certain dog at the exhibition which had, I said, obtained a medal. 'Not a medal,' she replied, 'but an honorable mention.' And then the dispute began, during which we jumped from one topic to another, reproaching each other at every step: 'Ah! yes, I knew that long ago; it's always so with you.' 'You said so yourself.' 'No, I said nothing of the kind.' 'I am a liar, then, I suppose,' and so on; and you feel that a minute more and a terrible struggle will begin, in which you would like to kill yourself or your antagonist. You know that it will begin presently, and you are in terror of it, and would like to restrain yourself, but hatred takes possession of your whole being. Her state was, if possible, still worse than mine; she deliberately put a wrong construction upon everything I said; and every word that she uttered herself was saturated with venom, and she was careful to prick my tender spots and reopen old sores, with every one of which she was perfectly familiar. As the dispute advanced matters grew worse. 'Silence!' I thundered at last, or some such exclamation to this effect. She rushes out of the room in the direction of the nursery, I following and striving to stop her in order that she should hear me out. As I seize her by the sleeve she pretends that I have hurt her, and screams out, 'Children, here's your father beating me!' On which I roar out, 'Don't tell lies!' To which she replies in the same high key, 'This is not the first time you've done it.' The children run up to her, and she calms them, while I continue, 'Don't make believe.' 'It's all make believe in your eyes. You are quite capable of killing a person and then saying that she only pretends to be dead. Oh, I've found you out by this time. This is what you are longing for.'

" 'I wish you were dead like a dog!' I shout out in reply. I remember how surprised and horrified I was when I uttered these terribly coarse words, and I can not explain how they could have passed my lips. As soon as I had pronounced them I ran out of the room into my study, sat down and began to smoke. From there I could hear her in the antechamber making ready to go out. I called out, 'Where are you going?' But she made no reply. 'The devil speed her!' I say to myself, as going back to my study, I lie down again and smoke. A thousand different plans of revenge crowded into my brain, and ingenious combinations by means of which

I was to make everything good again and repair what had been said and done. I ponder upon all this, smoking the while with all my might. It occurs to me to run away from her, to conceal myself, to emigrate to America; I actually go so far as to consider how I can best rid myself of her altogether, and please my fancy with the thought that after that consummation everything will again be as it should be, I shall then link myself to another lovely woman, fresh and pure; and the way of getting rid of her will be her natural death, or else I shall sue for a divorce; and then I mentally discuss with myself the best means of bringing this about. Then I become aware of the fact that I am wandering from the point at issue, that my thoughts are not what they should be, and in order to cloud my clear consciousness of this I smoke.

"Meanwhile, things at home were taking their usual course. The governess arrives and inquires, 'Where is madame? When will she return?' The lackey asks, 'Shall I serve the tea?' I repair to the dining-room; the children are there, and they look at me interrogatively, reproachfully, especially Liza, who is already beginning to understand the meaning of these things. We drink our tea in silence; *she* is not come yet. The whole evening passes away, and still she has not returned. Meanwhile, two different feelings alternately take possession of my soul: anger that she is torturing the children and me by her absence, the upshot of which will be that she will come back in the end; and fear that she will never return, that she will lay violent hands upon herself. I would go and fetch her, but where is she? At her sister's? But it would look so ridiculous for me to go there and make inquiries; and besides, I don't care; if she wants to pain me, then let her torment herself too. If I were to worry myself and run hither and thither to look for her, I should be merely playing into her hands, for that is just the end she had in view when she left the house, and she would thus be encouraged to do worse next time. But what if she be not at her sister's; what if she has in some way made away with herself? Eleven o'clock has struck. Twelve o'clock. I do not go into the bedroom; it would be stupid of me to lie down by myself there and wait. But even here in my study I do not lie down; I wish to undertake some kind of work that will occupy me—to write letters or to read, for instance; but I find that I am incapable of doing anything, and so I watch and wait by myself in my study, tormenting myself, boiling with rage, listening to every sound, real and imaginary. It is already three o'clock. It has struck four, and she is not yet come. Toward morning I fell asleep. When I awoke she had not returned. Meanwhile, everything in the household went on as before, only every one had a puzzled, dissatisfied air, and they all looked at me interrogatively and reproachfully, as if they felt that all this had been caused by me. And all this while my soul was the arena in which the same struggle for the mastery went on as before between anger at her having left me, and fear lest something had happened to her. At eleven o'clock her sister drove up as her envoy, and the old procedure was gone over again as if it were new. 'She is in a terrible state; what's it all about?' 'Nothing has happened.' I emphasize her impossible character, and affirm that I did nothing to her. 'Yes, but things can not remain as they now are, at all events,' her sister exclaims. 'That's her affair, not mine,' I answer. 'I will not make the first advances. If we are to separate, then let us separate.' And so her sister returned without having accomplished anything. I had said boldly that I would not move first in the matter, but as soon as she had gone, and I went out and saw the sad and frightened faces of the children, I was perfectly willing to take the first step. I began to walk to and fro as before, and to smoke. I drank vodka and wine at lunch, and attained thereby the object I had in view, which was to hide from myself the stupidity of my own position.

"About three o'clock she drove up herself. As she made no remark when she saw me, I inferred that she had resolved to make peace, and I told her that it was she who had provoked me with her reproaches, and thus originated the quarrel. She turned to me with a harsh, uncompromising look in her face, which bore traces of profound suffering, and intimated that she had come not to ask for terms, but to take away the children, as it was impossible for us to live any longer together. On this I began to explain that I was not to blame, that it was she who had lashed me into fury with her stinging reproaches. She again fixed her harsh, triumphant gaze upon me, and exclaimed, 'Say no more, you have repented.' To which I answered that I hated comedies. She then screamed out something which I did not catch, and rushed off to her room and turned the key in the door. I pushed the door several times, but elicited no reply. I then went off infuriated. Half an hour later Liza ran up to me in tears: 'What has happened? I can not hear mamma.' We go together to her room. I push the door, and the bolt being badly drawn, both of the folding-doors open at once, and I walk up to the bed. She is lying in an uncomfortable position on the bed, dressed in her petticoats and high boots; on the table by the bedside there is an empty bottle that has had opium in it. We bring her to herself, and tears follow closely on the first signs of returning consciousness, and everything winds up with a reconciliation. In our hearts, however, we foster the same hatred for each other, to which is superadded the feeling of exasperation caused by the pain and suffering that accompanied this quarrel, which each puts down to the account of the other. But it was indispensable to end this in one way or another, and life moves forward again in its old groove.

"And such quarrels as these, and still worse ones, were continually occurring; now once a week, now once a month, now every day. And always the same old story, without variations or modifications. Once things went so far that I applied for a foreign passport. That quarrel lasted two days; but it, too, finished with a half-hearted explanation and reconciliation, and I did not go abroad."

CHAPTER XXI
A STRANGE FATAL FORCE

"THIS IS THE sort of life we led, these were the relations in which we stood to each other when that man—Trookhatschevsky was his name—made his appearance. He came to Moscow and called upon me one morning. I bid the servant show him in. In former times he and I had been on terms of familiarity: now he felt his way carefully before venturing to treat me on the old footing, and employed expressions and spoke in a tone equally far removed from distant formality and the familiarity of comrades. I quickly solved his doubts by treating him as a mere acquaintance, and he took his cue readily, without a moment's hesitation or awkwardness.

"I disliked him exceedingly from the first moment I looked upon him. But some strange fatal force moved me not only to refrain from repelling him, but to draw him nearer to me. What could be simpler than to exchange a few words with him, to bid him good-bye chillingly, and not to introduce him to my wife? But no; I must talk about his playing, and tell him that I had heard he had given up music. He said it was not so; that he had never practiced more assiduously all his life than at that moment; and passing from himself to me, reminded me that I, too, had played in times gone by. To this I replied that I did not play now, but that my wife was a good musician. It is very curious! From the very first day, from the very first hour I saw him, my relations toward him were such as they could only have been subsequently to everything that occurred later on. There was something very strained in my intercourse with him; I took note of every word, every expression uttered by him or by myself, and invested them with a significance justified by nothing that I then knew. I introduced him to my wife, and the conversation at once turned upon music, and he proffered his services to accompany her on the violin. That morning, as during all that later period, my wife looked extremely elegant, seductive, and provokingly beautiful. It was evident that he pleased her from the very first; moreover, she was also delighted at the prospect of being accompanied on the violin by him—a pleasure which she relished so highly that she had hired a musician of one of the theaters to accompany her. This satisfaction was reflected in her looks; but as soon as her eyes met mine, she guessed my feelings, and instantaneously changed the expression of her face; and then began the game of mutual deception all round. I smiled graciously, and looked as if I were delighted.

"He, eyeing my wife as all immoral men look upon pretty women, pretended to be interested exclusively in the topic under discussion—that is to say, in the very thing that was utterly devoid of interest in his eyes. She endeavored to seem indifferent, but was disconcerted somewhat by that false smile on my face which denoted the jealous man and was quite familiar to her, and by his gaze. I saw that her eyes gleamed with a peculiar brightness from the moment she first saw him, and that owing, perhaps, to my jealousy an electric current seemed to connect them and establish uniformity in their looks and smiles; so that when she would blush he would blush, and as soon as she smiled he smiled also. We chatted a little about music, Paris, and various trivial commonplaces, and then he rose to leave, and smiling, with his hat pressed against his quivering thigh, stood looking now at her, then at me, as if waiting to see what we should do.

"I distinctly remember that moment, because during those short-lived seconds it lay in my power not to invite him to our house, and then that episode would never have occurred. But I glanced at him and at her: 'Do not for a moment delude yourself with the idea that I am jealous of you,' I mentally said to her, 'or that I have any fear of you,' I mentally said to him; and I thereupon asked him to come and see us in the evening, and to bring his violin with him, to accompany my wife. She looked at me in astonishment, blushed, and was fluttered and frightened, as it were, began to decline the offer, saying that she could not play well enough for that. This refusal of hers only irritated me, and I insisted the more strongly. I well recollect the strange feeling with which I looked at the back of his head and his white neck, set off by the black hair which was carefully combed back on both sides of his head, as with a frisky, saltatory motion, suggestive of the hopping of a bird, he walked out. I could not disguise from myself the fact that this man's presence was a torture to me; it is in my power, I said to myself, to act in such a way that we shall never be troubled by his visits any more. But to act thus is to admit that I go in fear of him. And I have not the slightest fear of him; that would be too degrading, I said to myself. And in the antechamber, as he was preparing to go, I insisted, knowing that my wife would hear everything I was saying, on his coming again in the evening, bringing his violin with him. This he promised to do, and left.

"In the evening he came, and they played together; but for a long time their play was inharmonious; they had not the music that my wife wanted, and she was unable to play without preparation the music they had. I was very fond of music myself, and I rather liked the idea of their playing together; and I arranged the music-stand and turned over the leaves for him. They managed at last to execute a few pieces: some songs without words and a sonata of Mozart. He played magnificently; for he possessed in the highest degree what is termed *ton*, over and above which he was endowed with a delicate, refined taste which seemed wholly out of harmony with his character. He played much better than my wife, of course, and assisted her, at the same time respectfully praising her play. She seemed interested only in the music, and behaved simply and naturally. As for me, although I pretended to be interested in the music, I was suffering indescribable torture from jealousy all the evening.

"What considerably augmented the pain I experienced was the knowledge that the only feeling she entertained for me was one of chronic irritation, only interrupted occasionally for a short while, as before; while, on the other hand, he was qualified by his elegant appearance, the fact that he was a new-comer, and, above all, by reason of his undoubted musical talent, to produce a profound impression on her. In virtue of all this, and also of the fact that they must necessarily be frequently thrown in each other's society by playing together, and, thanks to the influence of music, especially that of the violin, on impressionable natures, this man must not merely take her fancy, but conquer her completely. I could not help noticing all this, and I suffered horribly in consequence. And yet, in spite of this, or, rather, perhaps, by reason of it, an invisible power compelled me against my will to be not only extremely courteous, but affectionate toward him. I am unable to specify the motive which prompted me to act thus; whether it was to prove to my wife and to him that I was not actuated by fear, or to deceive myself, I can not say; I only know that from the very first my relations with him were not natural and unaffected.

"In order not to give myself up to the desire to kill him on the spot, I felt compelled to treat him cordially. I entertained him at supper with expensive wines, went into ecstasies over his musical talents, spoke to him with a peculiarly affectionate smile, and invited him to dinner on the following Sunday, and to accompany my wife in the evening. I said that I would ask some musical friends of mine to come and hear him. And so that day came to an end."

Here Pozdnischeff was overcome with emotion, and, changing his position, again made that peculiar noise.

"It is surprising how I was affected by the presence of that man," he resumed, manifestly putting forth a strong effort to compose himself. "I was returning from the Exhibition three or four days after this, and, on entering the house, I suddenly felt oppressed at heart, as if a heavy stone were weighing me down; and at first I saw nothing to account for the feeling. Then I remembered that it originated in my having descried something, as I was passing through the antechamber, which reminded me of *him*. It was only when I was in my study that I was conscious of what that something was, and I immediately returned to verify the discovery. Yes, I was not mistaken; it was his overcoat. You know, a fashionable great-coat. I was extremely sensitive to everything relating in any way to him, noticing it at once, even though I was not always distinctly conscious of it. I then asked the servant. Yes, he was there. I then went to my room, not through the parlor, but through the children's class-room. My daughter Liza was reading a book, and the nurse at the table with the youngest child was spinning the cover of some vessel. The door leading into the drawing-room was open, and I could hear the measured *arpeggio* and the sound of her voice and his. I listened, but could not distinguish any words. It was evident that the notes of the piano were evoked merely for the purpose of drowning their conversation—their kisses, perhaps. Good God! what a wild beast was roused up within me! What horrible imaginings thronged my mind! Even now I am filled with horror at the mere recollection of the fury that then took possession of my soul.

"My heart contracted, stopped, and then suddenly thumped against my breast like a sledge-hammer. The predominating feeling in this, as in all rage and hatred, was pity for myself. 'Before the children, before the nurse,' I said to myself. There must have been something terrible in my face, for Liza looked at me with terror reflected in her eyes. 'What am I to do?' I asked myself. 'To go in? I can not. God only knows what I shall do if I go in. And yet I can not go away!' The nurse looked at me as if she understood my position.

" 'I can not but go in,' I said to myself, and quickly threw open the door. He was seated at the piano practicing the *arpeggio* with his large white fingers turned upward; she stood at a corner of the piano, some open music spread out before her. She was the first to see or hear me, and she turned her eyes upon me. Was she frightened, and her external composure only simulated, or was she really composed? I can not say; but certain it is that she did not start or move in any way when I entered; she merely blushed; and even that was not till afterward.

" 'I am so glad you have come; we have not yet decided what to play next Sunday,' she said in a tone of voice that she would never have employed had we been alone. This and the 'we,' referring to him and herself, incensed me. I saluted him in silence; he shook me by the hand, and immediately went on to explain to me, with a smile that I considered derisive, that he had brought some music in order to prepare for Sunday, but that they were not agreed what to play; whether it was to be something difficult and classical—namely, one of Beethoven's sonatas, with the violin—or light, trivial pieces? All this was so simple and natural that I could not find anything to cavil at, and, at the same time, I saw and was convinced that it was wholly untrue, and that they had been concerting measures to play me false.

"There can be nothing more agonizing for jealous people—and in our social life all men are jealous—than certain of the conditions of fashionable life which render the closest and most dangerous contact between man and woman permissible. It is impossible, without making one's self the laughing-stock of the world, to hinder this proximity between men and women dancing at balls, between doctors and their women patients, between artists, painters, and musicians working together.

"Two persons are cultivating the noblest art—music—together; this requires a certain proximity, in which there is nothing unseemly, and no one but a stupid, jealous husband, forsooth, could find anything reprehensible therein. And yet every one knows full well that it is, thanks to these very occupations, especially musical studies, prosecuted together, that by far the greatest proportion of wickedness takes place in our society.

"It was clear that I disconcerted the pair by my own embarrassment: for a long time I could say nothing; I resembled a bottle turned up side down, from which the liquid can not escape, owing to the bottle being too full. I wanted to load them with reproaches, to expel him from the house, but I felt, on the other hand, that I ought to appear amiable and affectionate toward him. And I appeared so: I pretended to approve of everything—in obedience to the impulse that made me increase my outward civility and cordiality toward him in proportion as the mental sufferings caused by his presence grew more acute. I said that I felt perfect confidence in his taste, and I advised her to follow my example. He remained just as long as was absolutely necessary to remove the disagreeable impression which I had caused by suddenly walking into the room with a terrified face, and continuing to preserve an awkward silence after I had entered. Then he left, pretending that now they had determined what pieces they would execute on the morrow. I was persuaded that the question of the musical programme was utterly indifferent to them. I accompanied him with marked obsequiousness to the antechamber—how could I treat less courteously the man who had come to disturb the peace and ruin the happiness of my family?—and I pressed with unwonted warmth his soft white hand."

CHAPTER XXII
INSANE RAGE

"ALL THAT DAY I did not speak to my wife. I could not. Proximity to her produced such an upheaval of hatred within me that I was frightened of myself. At dinner she asked me in presence of the children when I intended to go to the country—I was obliged to go to the country the following week, to attend the district sittings of the Zemstvo.[1] I mentioned the date. She asked me whether I needed anything for the journey. I said not, and sat on in silence till the end of the dinner, and in silence rose up from the table and went to my study. Of late she never used to come to my room, especially at that time of day. I had lain down in my study, and was giving myself up to angry thoughts, when suddenly the horrid, absurd idea entered my head that she was coming to hide her sin—like Uriah's wife[2]—and that that was why she was about to call upon me at that unusual hour. 'Can it be that she is really coming to me?' I asked myself, as I heard her footsteps approaching nearer and nearer. 'If so, it is evident that I was right, then; she—' And I felt an inexpressible hatred for her. Nearer and still nearer; is it possible that she will not pass by and go into the drawing-room? No; the door suddenly creaked on its hinges, and there on the threshold stood her tall, well-proportioned, handsome figure, her face and eyes expressive of timidity, of a desire to ingratiate herself with me, a desire which she endeavored to conceal, but which did not escape my notice, and the meaning of which I well knew. I held my breath so long that I was nearly suffocated, and continuing to regard her, I caught hold of the cigarette-case and began to smoke.

" 'How can you, now? A person comes to sit down and have a quiet chat with you, and here you take out your cigarettes and smoke!' and she seated herself on the sofa beside me, leaning gently up against me. I moved a little further off, so as not to be in contact with her. 'I see that you are annoyed that I am going to play on Sunday?' she said. 'I'm not annoyed in the least,' I answered. 'Do you think I don't see it?' 'I can only congratulate you if you do. The only thing that I can see is, that you conduct yourself like a *cocotte*—'[3] 'Oh, if you want to abuse me in such language, I will go.' 'Go; but mark this, if the honor of the family is not dear to you, it is not you who are dear to me—the devil take you!—but

[1] [Local council.]
[2] [Bathsheba in the Bible, coveted by King David.]
[3] [Harlot.]

the honor of the family is.' 'What—what do you mean?' 'Leave the room; leave the room, for God's sake!' I do not know whether she only made believe that she did not understand me, or she really did not understand me, but she took offense. She rose, but did not go, and continued standing in the middle of the room: 'You are making yourself positively unbearable. You have a character that makes it impossible even for an angel to live with you;' and bent as usual upon stinging me in the most sensitive place, she reminded me of how I had once treated my sister. (I had once lost my temper and spoken very coarsely to my sister, and the recollection of this was always extremely painful to me. Hence she chose this sore place to prick me.) 'If you treat your own sister in that way, nothing that you could do would surprise me,' she concluded. 'Yes, she is not content with offending me, humiliating me, disgracing me, but she must make it appear that I am to blame for it all,' I said to myself; and I conceived such a consuming hatred for her as I had never in my whole life felt before. For the first time I longed to give my hatred physical expression. I started to my feet and moved toward her, but just as I was doing so I remember I became conscious that I was moved by angry passion, and I asked myself whether I was doing right to abandon myself to its power, and instantaneously came the answer that it was right, because that would terrify her, and so instead of withstanding, combating my rage, I began to fan it into a still more powerful flame, taking a peculiar delight in the contemplation of its rapid spread and growing intensity.

" 'Leave me, or I'll kill you!' I screamed; and going up to her I caught her by the arm. When pronouncing these words I deliberately pitched my voice in a higher key to express my anger; and no doubt I did look terrible, for she was so terror-stricken that she had not the force to leave the room. She only said: 'Vasa, what's the matter with you?' 'Leave me,' I vociferated still louder; 'only you can drive me mad; I can't answer for what may happen!'

"Having let loose my angry passion, I drank it in with inebriating delight, and I felt a desire to do something extraordinary, something which would mark the culminating point of my insane rage.

"I conceived an almost insuperable desire to beat her, to kill her, but I was aware that this could not be; therefore, in order to give loose reins to my rage, I seized the *presse-papier*[1] that lay on the table, and screaming out once more, 'Leave me!' I dashed it to the ground close to where she stood. I had carefully aimed so as to miss her. Thereupon she left the room, but remained standing on the threshold; and while she was still

[1] [Paperweight.]

looking at me—I did it expressly that she should look—I snatched up various articles that were on the table—the candle-stick, the ink-bottle—and flung them to the ground, continuing to cry out, 'Leave me! take yourself off! I can not answer for what I may do!' She left, and I instantaneously ceased. An hour later the nurse came and said that my wife was in hysterics. I went to her room; she was sobbing and laughing by turns; she could not speak a word, and her whole body trembled violently. She was not making believe, but was really ill.

"Toward morning she grew calm, and we made up the quarrel under the influence of that feeling which we call 'love.' In the morning, when, after the reconciliation, I confessed to her that I was jealous of Trookhatschevsky, she was not at all confused, but laughed in the most natural way conceivable—so queer did it seem to her, she said, that an attachment on her part for such a man should be deemed a possibility.

" 'Can such a man as he cause any other feelings in a respectable woman than pleasure at his musical performances? If you like, I am willing to refuse to see him any more, even on Sunday—although all the guests have been invited—write to say I am unwell, and there's an end to the matter. There is only one thing irritating about it—that is, that any one, especially that he himself, should for a moment suppose that he is dangerous. And I have too much pride to let anything of the kind be imagined.' And this was not a lie. She honestly believed what she was saying; indeed, she hoped by these words to evoke within herself a feeling of contempt for him, and by means of it to defend herself from his attacks. But she failed. Everything was against her, especially that accursed music.

"In this way the incident was wound up, and on Sunday the guests gathered together, and the two performed again."

CHAPTER XXIII
THE SONATA

"I DEEM IT superfluous to say that I was extremely vain. Life without vanity is become almost an impossibility. On Sunday I endeavored to the best of my power to give a *recherché*[1] dinner, and to arrange the *soirée musicale*[2] with taste and success. I even went out myself to purchase

[1] [Carefully planned and prepared.]
[2] [Evening party with musical entertainment.]

certain things for the dinner, and personally called on the guests. By six o'clock the guests had come, and he also was there in evening dress with diamond shirt studs of questionable taste. He seemed perfectly at his ease, replied to all questions hurriedly, with a smile of assent and approval, and with that peculiar expression which is meant to suggest that everything you say or do is precisely what he had been expecting. All his unfavorable traits and characteristics were noted by me with unusual satisfaction that evening, because they were calculated to tranquilize me and prove to me that the level on which he stood was too low for my wife, who could not degrade herself to stoop down to it. I did not permit myself to be jealous now. In the first place, I had suffered from the pangs of jealousy till the furthest limits of endurance were reached, and I now needed repose; and in the second place I desired to put faith in my wife's assurances, and I did put faith in them. But, although I was not at all jealous, yet, do what I would, I could not be natural in my intercourse with him and with her during the dinner, and all the first half of the evening until the music began. I was continually watching and scanning their movements and their looks. The dinner was, as dinners generally are, tedious, conventional. The music began at an early hour.

"Ah! how I remember all the circumstances, even the most trivial incidents, of that *soirée*; how he brought in his violin, opened the box, removed the covering, which had been worked for him by a lady, took out the instrument, and began to tune it; how my wife took her place at the piano with a look of indifference beneath which I could see that she concealed considerable diffidence, chiefly diffidence in her own powers; how, as soon as she was seated, the usual preparatory notes were extracted from the piano and the violin, the usual rustling sound of the music was heard as it was spread out on the stands; then how they looked at each other, glanced rapidly at the guests who were seating themselves, and began. He took the first chords, his face instantaneously becoming serious, severe, sympathetic, and, as he listened to the notes he was producing, he drew his fingers cautiously along the strings. The piano answered him, and the concert began."

Here Pozdnischeff stopped and uttered that peculiar sound of his several times in succession. He was about to resume his story, but merely snuffled, and lapsed again into silence. After a pause he went on.

"They played the 'Kreutzer Sonata' of Beethoven; do you know the first *presto*? Eh? Ah! . . ." he exclaimed, "it is a strange piece of music, that sonata, especially the first part of it. And music generally is a strange thing. I can not comprehend it. What is music? What effect does it produce? And in virtue of what does it produce the effect that we see it produce?

"Music, they say, acts on one by elevating the soul. That is absurd. It acts upon us, it is true, acts with terrible effect—at least I am speaking for myself—but is far from elevating the soul. It neither elevates nor depresses the soul, but irritates it. How shall I make my meaning clear? Music forces me to forget myself and my true state; it transports me to some other state which is not mine. Under its influence I fancy I experience what I really do not feel, that I understand what I do not comprehend, that I am able to do what is completely beyond my power. I explain this by the supposition that music acts like yawning or laughing; thus, although not sleepy, I yawn if I see others yawning; although I see nothing to laugh at I burst out laughing simply if I hear others laughing. Music instantaneously throws me into that state of feeling in which the composer of it found himself when he wrote it. My soul blends with his, and together with him I am transported from one frame of mind to another. But why I am so ravished out of myself I know not. He who composed the piece—Beethoven, for instance, in the case of the 'Kreutzer Sonata'—knew perfectly well why he was in that mood; it was that mood that determined him to do certain things, and therefore for him that state of mind has a meaning; for me it has absolutely none. This is why it is that music only causes irritation, never ends anything. It is a different thing if a military march is played; then the soldiers move forward, keeping time to the music, and the end is attained; if dance music is played, people dance to it, and the object is also accomplished; if a mass is sung, I receive Holy Communion, and here, too, the music is not in vain; but in other cases there is nothing but irritation, and no light how to act during this irritation. Hence the terrible effects that music occasionally produces. In China music is a state concern, and this is as it ought to be. Could it be tolerated in any country that any one who takes the fancy may hypnotize any one else and then do with him whatever he has a mind to, especially if this magnetizer is—Heaven knows who!—an immoral character, for instance?

"It is indeed a terrible weapon in the hands of those who know how to employ it. Take the 'Kreutzer Sonata,' for example: is it right to play that first *presto* in a drawing-room to ladies in low dresses? to play that *presto*, then to applaud it, and immediately afterward to eat ice creams and discuss the latest scandal? Such pieces as this are only to be executed in rare and solemn circumstances of life, and even then only if certain important deeds that harmonize with this music are to be performed. It is meant to be played and then to be followed by the feats for which it nerves you; but to call into life the energy of a sentiment which is not destined to manifest itself by any deed, how can that be otherwise than baneful?

"Upon me, at least, this piece produced a terrible effect; it seemed as if new feelings were revealed to me, new possibilities unfolded to my gaze, of which I had never even dreamed before. 'It is thus that I should live and think, and not as I have hitherto lived and thought,' a voice seemed to whisper in my soul. What that new object of knowledge was, I could not satisfactorily explain to myself; but the consciousness of its existence was most delightful. All the people whom I knew, my wife and he among the number, appeared to me in an entirely new light. After this *presto* they executed the splendid but traditional *andante*, which has nothing new in it, with the commonplace variations and very weak *finale*. Then, at the request of the guests, they performed an elegy of Ernst and several other light pieces, all of them excellent in their way, but which did not make even the one hundredth part of the impression on me which the first piece produced. I was cheerful and good-humored for the rest of the evening. I had never before seen my wife as she appeared to me that evening: those gleaming eyes, that severity and gravity of mien while she played, that dissolving languor, and that soft, melting, blissful smile that played over her features when they had finished. I saw all that, but put no other construction upon it than that she was undergoing the same experience as myself; that feelings new and never before experienced were revealed to her—brought dimly within the range of her consciousness. The *soirée*, which was a complete success, came to an end at last, and the guests took their leave.

"Knowing that I should have to leave for the interior in two days' time, Trookhatschevsky said, as he was bidding me good-night, that the next time he came he hoped to renew the pleasure he had experienced that evening. I inferred from this that he did not deem it possible to visit my house in my absence, and this gave me satisfaction. It was clear that as I should not return before his departure from Moscow, we should not see each other any more. For the first time I shook his hand with unfeigned pleasure, and thanked him for the treat. He also took a final leave of my wife, and their leave-taking appeared to me in the highest degree natural and correct. My wife and myself were both quite delighted with the *soirée*."

CHAPTER XXIV
CONSUMMATION

"TWO DAYS AFTERWARD I departed for the country in the calmest and happiest frame of mind, after having taken leave of my wife. In the country I had always found plenty of work awaiting me, and a new life, an original little world, different from the one in which I usually lived. I worked for ten hours a day, two days in succession, in the department. The day after my arrival in the country I was sitting in the department, engaged in my work, when a letter from my wife was delivered to me. I opened and read it there and then. She wrote about the children, about her uncle, the nurse, about various purchases which she had made, and added at the fag end, and as if it were a most trivial circumstance, 'Trookhatschevsky has called and brought the music that he promised me, and offered to play again, but I declined.' Now, I had no recollection of his having promised to bring any music, and I certainly had the impression that he had taken leave forever, and this piece of news was consequently extremely disagreeable to me. But I had so much to attend to just then that I had no spare time to think the matter over, and it was only in the evening, when I had got back to my lodging, that I read the letter over again. Besides, the circumstance that Trookhatschevsky had called in my absence, the whole tone of the letter appeared to me enigmatical. The furious wild beast of jealousy within me roared in his den and endeavored to escape thence; but, fearing he might succeed, I made haste to shut the door.

" 'What an odious feeling this jealousy is!' I said to myself, 'and what could be more natural than what she writes?' And I went to bed and commenced to think about the affairs that I should have to take in hand the next day. During these sittings of the Zemstvo I never could go asleep very soon, owing partly, no doubt, to the unfamiliar place; this night, however, I very quickly fell asleep.

"And as often happens in such cases I felt something in the nature of an electric shock and suddenly awoke. I awoke thinking of her, of my love for her, and of Trookhatschevsky. Horror and rage crushed my heart between them; but I strove to listen to the promptings of reason. 'What absurd suspicions!' I said to myself; 'there's not the shadow of a foundation for them. And how can I thus degrade my wife? Here on the one hand is a fellow who might almost be described as a hired fiddler, known to be disreputable, and on the other an estimable, respected mother of a family—*my* wife. How preposterous!' This was one current of ideas. There was also another; and the thoughts that composed it were very different: 'Why should it not happen? What incongruity is there in supposing that such a natural and intelligible thing may have occurred? He is not married, well-fed, sleek, and not only devoid of principle, but guided by the rule that one should enjoy whatever pleasures one finds in one's way. And between these two beings there is the connecting bond of music—the most refined lust of the senses. What considerations are likely to keep him in bounds? None. On the contrary, everything conspires to attract him. And she? What is she? She is the mystery that she ever was. I do not know her. I know her only as a creature of instinct. And nothing is capable of restraining a creature of instinct.

"It was only at that moment that I called to mind their faces as I saw them that memorable Sunday evening when, after they had executed the 'Kreutzer Sonata,' they played some little piece, I forget by whom, I only remember that it was passionate to excess. 'How could I have been foolish enough to leave the city?' I asked myself as I called their faces to mind. 'Was it not as clear as daylight that everything was consummated between them on that evening; was it not manifest that on that evening not only was there no barrier subsisting between them, but that they both, especially she, felt some little shame at the recollection of what had taken place between them? I recollect how she smiled feebly, tenderly, and blissfully, wiping the perspiration from her flushed face, as I approached the piano. Already then they avoided looking at each other, and it was only at supper, when he was pouring her out some water, that they glanced at each other and smiled almost imperceptibly. I now shuddered when the look that I caught on their faces came back to my mind, accompanied as it was by that feeble smile. 'Yes, everything is now consummated,' one voice whispered into my ear. 'You are half demented; don't you know that that can not be?' exclaimed the other voice. There was something very weird and ghastly, it seemed to me, in my lying there in the darkness, a prey to these thoughts; so I struck a match, and all at once a feeling of indescribable dread came over me, as I looked around me in that little room with the yellow wallpapers. I lighted a cigarette, and as it always occurs to you to smoke when you are moving round and round, as I was, in the same circle of insoluble contradictions, I smoked cigarette after cigarette for the purpose of clouding my reason and avoiding the sight of the contradictions. I did not fall asleep any more that night, and at five o'clock, having come to the conclusion that I would no longer remain in that state of mental tension, I got out of bed, called the door-keeper who usually waited upon me, and sent him for the horses. I scribbled a note to the department, to say that I had been summoned to Moscow on very urgent business, and to request that, in the meanwhile, my place be temporarily taken by another member. At eight o'clock I took my seat in the tarantass[1] and drove off. . . ."

[1] [Another type of carriage.]

CHAPTER XXV
ABSORPTION

THE CONDUCTOR ENTERED the carriage, and perceiving that our candle had burned down to the socket, blew it out, without lighting another. Day was already breaking. Pozdnischeff was silent, sighing heavily from time to time, until the conductor again went out, leaving us in obscurity. Nothing was audible but the clinking of the glass windows, the rumblings and creaking of the rolling carriages, and the regular, monotonous snore of the clerk. In the uncertain gray of the dawn, I could not distinguish the figure of Pozdnischeff; but his voice grew louder as it became more piteous and excited.

"I had to drive thirty miles in the tarantass and then travel eight hours by rail. The drive was magnificent. It was a frosty autumn morning with bright, cheerful sunshine; the roads were smooth, the rays of the sun brilliant, and the air bracing. The riding in the tarantass was pleasant. As soon as day broke and I set out, I felt eased at heart. Looking at the horses, the fields, the people on foot we met, made me forget whither I was bound. At times it seemed as if I were only out for a drive, and that none of the circumstances that had combined to make me undertake the journey had ever had any existence in reality. And I felt a peculiar pleasure in thus forgetting myself. Whenever I did recollect on what errand I was bound, I said to myself, 'Don't think about that now; we'll see afterward what's to be done.' When we got half-way to the station, an incident occurred which stopped my progress and distracted me still more from my thoughts—the tarantass broke down and had to be mended. This accident was of still greater importance than was at first apparent, inasmuch as it occasioned the delay on the road which prevented my catching the express, and so I had to wait some hours and go on with the passenger train, thus getting into Moscow not, as I had intended, at five o'clock, but at midnight, thus reaching my own house toward one o'clock. The drive over, the search of a country wagon, the work of repairing, the payment, tea at the inn, and my conversation with the doorkeeper—all these things diverted my thoughts from what might otherwise seem their natural channel. By dusk, everything was ready, and I resumed my journey, which was still more pleasant after dark than during the day. There was a young moon, a slight frost, a splendid road, a jovial driver; and I drove forward, scarcely once reverting in thought to what was awaiting me; or was it that I enjoyed myself so thoroughly precisely because I knew what I had to expect, and was taking leave of all the joys of life? At all events this calm state of mind and the power of controlling my feelings came to an end with the drive in the tarantass.

"The moment I entered the train the conditions changed completely. This eight hours' journey in a railway carriage was a terrible experience for me, something I shall never forget to my dying day. Whether it was that having once taken my seat in the train I realized in a more lively manner than before that I was nearing the goal of my journey, or that railway traveling in general produces feverishness and unrest, I can not decide; I only know that from the moment I entered the compartment I lost all control over my imagination, which went on without cease, painting in the most vivid colors an endless series of pictures one after the other, one more cynical than the other, and all of a nature to inflame my jealousy, all treating the one theme—the doings that were going on at home in my absence, and how she was proving false to me. I was consumed with indignation, hatred, and a strange feeling of inebriation produced by my very dishonor, as I contemplated these pictures; powerless to tear myself away from them, unable to avoid looking at them, impotent to rub them out, too passive to hinder them from rising up before me. Nay, more, the longer I looked at them the more firmly did I believe in their reality. The life-like vividness with which these pictures presented themselves to my mind seemed to stamp with the impress of truth the scenes they delineated, and thus the phantoms of my brain succeeded in assuming all the appearance of reality. It seemed as if against my will some devil were employed in fabricating and suggesting to me the most horrible fancies and conjectures. A conversation that I had had many years before with Trookhatschevsky's brother recurred to me now, and applying it to Trookhatschevsky himself and my wife, I employed it to lacerate my heart. Trookhatschevsky's brother—although it had happened many years previously, it all came back to me now with great distinctness—in answer to the question whether he went to irregular places, replied that he did not, seeing that one could always establish relations in good society. And here now this man's brother had established relations with my wife. 'No, this thing is impossible!' I would then say to myself, terrified: 'It can not, can not be! Nay, there are not the slenderest grounds for supposing anything of the kind. Did she not herself assure me that she regarded the very possibility of my being jealous of him as dishonoring? She certainly did; but then she lies; yes, she is always lying,' I exclaimed, and thereupon everything began again *da capo*.[1] There were only two passengers in the compartment—an old woman and her husband, both of them very silent, and even they got out at one of the

[1] [From the beginning.]

intermediate stations, and I remained alone. I was exactly like a wild beast in a cage; now I would suddenly jump up and run to the window; then, reeling to the middle of the compartment, I would begin to pace rapidly forward as if trying to overtake the railway carriage; and the carriage with all its seats and windows went on shivering and shaking, just as ours is doing at this moment."

And here Pozdnischeff started to his feet, paced up and down for a few seconds, and then sat down again.

"Oh, how I fear, how I fear these railway carriages! They fill me with dread.

"Yes, it was a terrible time," he resumed. "I would say to myself, 'Come, I must think of something else. Let it be the proprietor of the road-side inn where I drank tea to-day.' And then before the eyes of my imagination I would see the door-keeper rising up, with his long beard, and his grandson, a little boy of the same age as my Vasa. My Vasa! My Vasa will see how a musician kisses his mother! What will take place in his poor soul at the sight? But what does she care? She is in love, forsooth. . . . And the whole thing began again. 'No, no! Let me think of the inspection of the hospital; yes, yesterday, I recollect, a patient complained of the doctor—the doctor with the mustaches like Trookhatschevsky's. How shamelessly, how impudently he deceived me—they both deceived me—when he said that he was going to leave Moscow!' And then the same racking thoughts began again. There was no subject that I could think of that was not in some way connected with them. I suffered terribly. What tormented me most was the uncertainty, the doubt, the vacillation, the ignorance I was in, whether I ought to love or hate her. My anguish was so excruciating that I remember it occurred to me to go on to the line, lie down on the rails, let the train pass over me, and end my pains. And the idea pleased me, for then, at least, I reflected, I should be troubled no more with torturing doubts. The only consideration that prevented me from acting on this impulse was pity for myself, which in turn, instantaneously called forth hatred toward her. Toward him I had a very strange feeling of hatred, mingled with the consciousness of my humiliation and his triumph; but for her my hatred was terrible. 'I can not make away with myself, and leave her behind me,' I said to myself; 'it is only right that she should suffer somewhat, that she should at least feel that I have suffered.'

"I got out at all the stations on the way to seek for distractions. At one station I saw people drinking in the refreshment-room, and I at once went up and poured myself out some vodka. A Jew stood beside me at the counter, and entered into conversation with me; and in order not to be quite alone in my carriage, I followed him to his third-class compartment, filthy though it was, reeking with stale tobacco smoke, and littered over with the husks of sunflower seeds; and I sat down on the wooden bench beside him. He was relating a number of anecdotes to me, which I did not understand nor even hear, because I continued to think of what was absorbing my own mind. He noticed this, and began to demand my attention to what he was saying, and then I got up and went back again to my own carriage. 'I must think it all over again,' I said to myself, 'I must sift and compare all the *pros* and *cons*, and see whether there is really any ground for the anguish I am causing myself.' And I sat down with the intention of weighing the matter calmly in my mind, but that very instant, instead of a calm analysis, the old train of thoughts was started afresh, and in lieu of arguments I saw the old pictures and imaginings.

" 'How often have I tortured myself,' I then thought, 'exactly in the same way before'—I here called to mind my former paroxysms of jealousy—'and all utterly groundless, as it afterward proved! It may be that my present suspicions are equally groundless—indeed, I am sure they are; when I get home I shall find her asleep, and by her words and looks I shall feel that nothing wrong has taken place, and that it was all a phantom of my brain. Oh, how delightful that would be!' 'But no, it has been so too often; this time it will assuredly be otherwise,' an interior voice seemed to say, . . . and the flood of bitter, corroding thoughts rushed in upon me again. Yes, that was in truth a torture! It is not, I thought, into a hospital that I would take a young man to show him the results of evil-doing, but into my own soul, to let him glance at the devils that are tearing it to pieces! A very revolting feature in all this was, that I was convinced I possessed an indefeasible right to my wife, just as if she were myself, and at the same time I felt that I could not possess her, that she was not mine, and that she could dispose of herself as she liked, and that she was minded to dispose of herself in a manner that I did not approve. And I could do nothing to him, and still less to her. 'If she has not deceived me, but is bent upon deceiving me—and I know perfectly well that she is so bent—the situation is still worse; it would be much better if she did deceive me, so that I should know for certain what to think, and get rid of all these horrid doubts and fears.' I could not formulate what I wanted or desired. It was madness pure and simple."

CHAPTER XXVI
SHE IS—

"At the last station but one, when the guard came in to collect the tickets, I got all my things together, and went out on the platform where the brake is worked; and standing there, the consciousness that the consummation was near only intensified my feverishness. I felt a sensation of extreme cold, which was soon followed by the chattering of my teeth. We reached our destination at last, and I left the station mechanically with the crowd, called a drosky, took my place, and drove home. During the ride home I gazed at the rare passers-by, the door-keepers of the houses, and the shadows projected by the vehicle now before, now behind, thinking of nothing the while. When we had gone about half a mile from the station, my feet became extremely cold, and I remembered that I had taken off my woolen stockings in the train, and put them in my traveling-bag. Where was my traveling-bag? Was it there in the drosky? It was. And where was the trunk? Then I became aware that I had forgotten all about my luggage; but having searched for and found the receipt for it, I decided that it was not worth my while to go back for it now; so I drove on. I have never been able since then to recall the state of mind in which I was during that drive home from the station. What were my thoughts? What were my wishes? All that is now an utter blank.

"I only remember that I was conscious that something terrible was brewing, an event of extreme importance in my life impending. Whether that important thing was taking place because I thought thus, or because I foreboded it, I can not say. It may be that after that which subsequently happened, all the moments that immediately preceded it were tinged with dismal hues in my memory.

"I drove up to the door. It was near one o'clock. A few cabmen were stationed before the street door waiting for fares—a reasonable expectation enough, to judge by the light in the windows—in our lodgings the windows of the drawing-room and parlor were brilliantly lighted up. Without attempting to explain to myself why the light was burning in our rooms at such a late hour, I walked up the doorsteps in that same state of expectancy—foreboding something terrible—and rang the bell. George, the lackey, a good, zealous, but extremely stupid man, opened the door. The first thing that struck me in the antechamber was the great-coat hanging from the clothes-rack along with other hats and coats. I ought to have been astonished at this, but I did not feel the least surprise, because I expected it. 'Just what I thought,' was the mental commentary I made when, in reply to my question, 'Who is here?' George mentioned the name of Trookhatschevsky. 'Any one else?' I asked. 'No, no one else.' I remember the tone of voice in which he said this, as if he were desirous of giving me pleasure and dispelling my apprehensions that there might be somebody else there. 'Exactly,' I muttered, as if aloud to myself; 'and the children?' 'The children, thank God, are well. They have been asleep ever so long, sir.' I could not breathe out freely, nor could I stop the chattering of my teeth. 'So,' I said to myself, 'it is not then as I thought it might be.' Hitherto I had been wont to imagine misfortunes, only to find that I had been mistaken, and that all was well. This time it is not as of yore: I am now face to face in grim reality with all that existed in my imagination, and, as I believed, only in my imagination. Here I find it all perfectly life-like and real.

"I was on the point of sobbing aloud, but at that moment the devil whispered: Whine and pule, give yourself up to sickly sentimentality, and give them time to separate, and then pass your life in heart-corroding doubts and torments. And all at once tenderness for myself disappeared, and was succeeded by a strange feeling: you will scarcely believe it—a feeling of joy that my torture was about to come to an end, that I could punish her now, rid myself of her, give loose reins to my hatred. And I did let loose my hatred, and it metamorphosed me into a wild beast, a malignant, cunning, savage beast. 'Stop! stop!' I cried to George, who was about to go into the parlor; 'look here; take a drosky and drive over to the station as quickly as ever you can and get my luggage. Here's the receipt. Lose no time.' He went along the corridor to get his overcoat. Apprehensive lest he should disturb the pair, I accompanied him to his little room and stood by while he was putting his great-coat on. Through the parlor, from which I was separated by another room, came the sound of voices and the noise of knives and plates. They were evidently eating, and had not heard the bell. 'I pray Heaven they may not leave the room yet!' I mentally ejaculated. George at last put on his coat and departed. I let him out and shut the door behind him, and I was seized with a weird, shuddering feeling when I saw myself quite alone and bound to act quickly. To act how? I did not know yet; I only knew that it was all over then, that there could be no longer any doubts about her guilt, that I would punish her presently, and break off all relations with her forever. Heretofore I had had hesitations; I had said to myself, 'Perhaps it is not true, perhaps I am mistaken.' I did not say or think so now; everything was decided once for all, irrevocably. 'Alone with him, without my knowledge, and at night! This argues complete forgetfulness of everything.' Or still worse: 'This audacity was adopted as the result of cool calculation; this assurance in committing crime was relied upon as a proof of innocence.' It is all perfectly clear. There can be no manner of doubt about it. The only thing I felt any uneasiness about was that they might escape, might hit upon some new way to baffle and deceive me, and might thus deprive me of the evidence of my senses, the possibility of proving their crime.

"And in order to lose no time in coming upon them and catching them, I went to the drawing-room where they were sitting, not through the parlor, but along the corridor and through the nursery, walking on the tips of my toes. In the first of the two rooms of which the nursery was composed the boys were sound asleep. In the second the nurse stirred and moved as if she were about to awake, and I had a very vivid presentiment of what she would think if she knew what was going on. I was thereupon filled with such profound pity for myself that I could not hold back my tears, and in order not to wake the child, I ran back along the corridor on the tips of my toes to my study, where I flung myself on the sofa and sobbed aloud.

"I, an honest man, the son of such respectable parents; I, who all my life cherished the dream of domestic happiness in the bosom of my family; I, her husband, who was never unfaithful to her—I have lived to see this thing! She, the mother of five children, and to throw herself into the arms of a musician because he has rosy lips! No, she is not a human being, she is . . . And all this in the room next the nursery where the children are, the children whom she has all her life been pretending to love. And then again to send me such a letter as she sent me! Nay, how do I know?—possibly this has been going on for ever so long. Had I come to-morrow, instead of to-night, she would have met me, her hair tastefully done up, her slender waist becomingly set off, with her languid, graceful movements, and the wild beast of jealousy imprisoned forever within me would have torn my heart to pieces. What will the nurse think? and George? and poor little Liza? (She was already of an age to understand something of what was going on.) 'And this shamelessness! this hypocrisy!' I exclaimed to myself.

"I wanted to rise, but I could not. My heart beat so violently that I could not stand on my feet. 'I shall have a fit and drop down dead,' I thought. 'She will indeed be the death of me. That's what she wants; killing would be nothing to her. But no, my death would be too much of a godsend to her; I must not give her this pleasure. Why, here am I sitting in my room while this very moment they are eating and laughing. . . . Oh, why did I not strangle her then?' I asked myself, as I called to mind the moment, a week ago, when I thrust her out of my study and smashed the things on the table. I had a most lively recollection of the state of mind I was in at that time; and not merely a recollection, but I experienced the very same desire to beat, to destroy, that animated me then. I remember how I burned to do something, to act, and how all considerations, except those that were indispensable for action, vanished from my mind in a twinkling, and I was left in a mood identical with that of a wild beast or of a human being under the influence of physical excitement in time of danger when a man naturally acts with precision, not hurriedly, yet without losing a single moment, and all with a single, definite object in view."

CHAPTER XXVII
HER LOOKS BETRAY

"THE FIRST THING I did was to take off my boots, and then in my stockings I went to the wall where my guns and daggers were suspended above the sofa, and took down a crooked Damascus blade that had never been used, and was exceedingly sharp. I unsheathed it. The scabbard slipped from my hands and fell down behind the sofa, and I remember saying to myself, 'I must look for it afterward, or it may get lost.' Then I divested myself of my great-coat, which I had worn all the time, and, stepping out softly in my stockings, I went *there*; and, stealing up inaudibly I suddenly threw open the door.

"I remember the expression of their faces. I remember it because at the time it afforded me an excruciating pleasure. It was an expression of terror, and that was precisely what I desired. To my dying day I shall not forget the regard of mingled despair and terror that was visible on their faces the first moment they beheld me. He was seated, I think, at the table, and as soon as he saw me he started to his feet and stationed himself with his back leaning against the cupboard. His features were expressive of unmistakable abject terror. Her face wore the same expression; but there was something else there besides; and had it not been for that something else, had I discovered no trace of anything but terror, perhaps that which happened a little later would have never taken place at all. For an instant, and only for an instant, her looks betrayed her—to my thinking, at least—the disappointment, the vexation she felt at being disturbed, at having the happiness which his society gave her broken in upon. She seemed to have but one thought, but one wish—namely, to be left alone to enjoy her happiness unmolested. Both of those expressions lingered but a second on their faces; his was instantaneously replaced by an interrogative glance at her which plainly said, 'Is it possible to right things by lying? If so, then it is time to begin. If not, something else will take place; but what?' Her look of vexation and disappointment was succeeded, I fancied, the moment her eyes met his, by solicitude for him. For an instant I stood on the threshold, holding the dagger behind my back, and that instant he smiled and began to speak in a tone of voice so studiously unconcerned that it seemed positively comical. 'And we were at our music—' he began.

" 'Well, this is a surprise!' she exclaimed the same moment, following up the cue he had given her.

"But neither he nor she finished what they were going to say. The insane frenzy that I had felt a week previously had again taken possession of me; once more I experienced the same mania for destroying, for using violence, for assuring the triumph of madness; and I yielded myself up to it body and soul.

"They never finished the sentences they had begun. That other alternative happened which he was so greatly afraid of, and it swept away in a trice all that they were going to say. I threw myself upon her, hiding all the time the dagger lest he should hinder me from plunging it into her side, under her breast. (I chose this spot from the very first.) Just as I was flinging myself upon her, he saw what I was about, and—what surprised me very much from him—caught me by the arm, and shouted out at the top of his voice, 'Think of what you are doing! Help!'

"I freed my arm and rushed upon him without uttering a word. His eyes encountering mine, he all at once turned as pale as a sheet, his very lips became bloodless and white, his eyes glistened with an unwonted luster, and—what likewise surprised me very much—he dived under the piano and fled from the room.

"I rushed after him, but felt a heavy weight suspended from my left arm. It was she. I struggled, and tried to tear myself from her; but she weighed me down still more heavily, and effectually prevented me from moving. This unlooked-for hindrance, the dragging weight, and her touch, from which I shrunk as from a loathsome thing, served only to inflame me still more. I felt that I was perfectly raging, and that I could not but appall her, and I exulted in the thought.

"Striking backward with my left arm with all the force I could gather, I hit her with my elbow in the face. She screamed and let go my arm.

"I was on the point of running out in pursuit of him, when it occurred to me that it would be ridiculous to rush off in my stockings after the lover of my wife, and I did not wish to be ridiculous, but to be terrible. Notwithstanding the irrepressible fury that was driving me, I was conscious all the time of the impression I produced on others. At times, indeed, that impression served to guide me.

"I turned round to her. She had fallen on the couch, and, holding her hands up to her bruised eyes, was looking at me. Her face was expressive of terror and of hatred for me, her enemy; it was just such a look as a rat might give when the trap in which he has been caught is being raised up to the light. At least I saw nothing but fear and hatred in her features, just such fear and hatred for me which love for another would inevitably call forth in her. Still, I might perhaps have restrained myself yet, and might not have done what I did, if she had only remained silent.

"But all at once she began to speak and to clutch at my hand, the hand that held the dagger.

" 'Think of what you are doing. Nothing has passed between him and me, nothing. I swear to you! Nothing.' I might still have wavered had it not been for those concluding words, from which I inferred that the opposite was true, that everything had taken place. These words required a reply. And the reply would have to correspond to the state of frenzy up to which I had lashed myself, and which went on *crescendo*, and would still go on gaining in intensity. Fury has its laws as well as other mental states.

" 'Do not lie, hell-hag!' I screamed, seizing her arm with my left hand. But she wrenched herself away from my grasp. Then, without relinquishing my hold of the dagger, I caught her with my left hand by the throat, threw her over on her back, and began to strangle her. How tough her neck seemed! She seized my arms with both her hands, tearing them away from her throat; and, as if I had only been waiting for this, I struck the dagger with all the strength I could muster, into her left side, under the ribs. . . .

"Whenever people assert that in a paroxysm of madness they do not remember what they are doing, they are either talking nonsense—or lying. I knew very well what I was doing, and did not for a single second cease to be conscious of it. The more I fanned the flame of my fury, the brighter burned within me the light of consciousness, lighting up every nook and corner of my soul, so that I could not help seeing everything I was doing. I can not affirm that I knew in advance what I was going to do, but the very moment I was doing anything, I fancy some seconds beforehand, I was conscious of what I was doing, in order, as it were, that I might repent of it in time, that I might afterward have it to say that I could have stayed my hand. Thus, I was aware that I was striking her below the ribs, and that the blade would penetrate. The moment I was doing this, I knew that I was doing something terrible, a thing I had never done before, an action that would be fraught with frightful consequences. But that consciousness was instantaneous, like a flash of lightning, and the deed followed so close upon it as to be almost simultaneous with it. My consciousness of the deed and of its nature was painfully distinct. I felt and still remember the momentary resistance of the corset, and of something else, and then the passage of the knife cutting its way through the soft parts of the body. She seized the dagger with both her hands, wounding them, but without staying its progress.

"Afterward, in prison, when a moral revolution had already worked radical changes in my being, I would ponder for hours at a time on the thoughts and sensations that had filled my mind during that fatal instant, recalling all possible details. I remember that a second, but barely a second, before the act was accomplished, I was terribly conscious that I was killing, that I had killed, a woman, a defenseless woman, my own wife. I recollect the indescribable horror of this state of mind, and I infer from it, and in fact I may add that I have a dim remembrance, that having plunged the dagger into her body, I instantaneously drew it out again, anxious thereby to remedy what I had done, to stay my hand. I then stood motionless for an instant, waiting to see what would happen, and whether it was possible to undo it.

"She suddenly sprung to her feet and screamed out: 'Nurse, he has murdered me!' The nurse, having heard the noise, was already on the threshold. I was still standing motionless, expectant, incredulous. Suddenly the blood welled forth from under her corset.

"Then I saw that what I had done was past remedying, and the same instant I decided that it was not desirable that it should be remedied, that this very thing was what I wanted to do, and what ought to have been done. I lingered on still, till she fell, and the nurse exclaiming 'God! God!' ran to her assistance; it was only then that I flung away the dagger and quitted the room. 'I must not get excited; I must think of what I am doing,' I said to myself, not looking at her or the nurse.

"The nurse began to scream and call the maid.

"I walked along the corridor, sent the maid to her mistress, and went to my room. 'What must I do now?' I asked myself—and the answer at once suggested itself. Going into my study, I went up to the wall, took down the revolver, examined it—it was loaded—and placed it on the table. I next picked up the scabbard from behind the sofa, and then seated myself on the sofa. I remained thus seated for a long time, thinking of nothing, recollecting nothing. I was conscious, however, of a considerable stir in the other rooms. I heard a vehicle driving up to the door with some one, then another. Then I heard and saw George coming into my study with my luggage—as if any one wanted it! 'Did you hear what has happened?' I asked him. 'Tell the house-porter to go and inform the police.'

"He went out without making any reply. I rose from the sofa, took out my cigarettes and the matches, and began to smoke. Before I had finished one cigarette I was overcome by drowsiness and fell asleep.

"I slept for about two hours. I dreamed that she and I were living on terms of affection; that we had quarreled, but were making it up, and that there was some little obstacle in the way, but that at bottom we were friends.

"I was awakened by a knocking at the door.

" 'That is the police,' I thought; 'I fancy I murdered her. But perhaps it is she herself who is knocking, and that nothing at all has happened.' The knocking at the door went on. I did not answer it, but strove to decide the question, Had all that really taken place or not? Yes, it had. I remembered the resistance of the corset, and the passage of the blade through the body, and the recollection sent an icy cold chill along my back, and made my flesh creep. . . .

"Yes, it had taken place. There was no mistake about that. Now it's my turn, I thought, to lay hands upon myself; but while I was still saying that to myself, I knew that I would not kill myself. And yet I rose and took up the revolver again. It seemed strange; I remember how many times before that I had been on the point of committing suicide—the night before, in the train, for instance—and it had always seemed to me such an easy thing to do; it had seemed easy, because I considered that to be the most effectual means of striking terror into her. But now not only could I not take my own life, but I could not even harbor the thought. 'Why should I kill myself?' I asked. And no answer was forthcoming. The knocking at the door continued. 'Ah, yes, I must first see who is at the door. There will be always time enough for this,' I thought, as I laid the revolver down on the table and covered it over with a newspaper. I then went to the door, and drew back the bolt. It was my wife's sister, a well-meaning, silly widow.

" 'Vasa, what's all this?' she exclaimed, and the tears—always ready with her—flowed abundantly.

" 'What do you want?' I asked, gruffly. I knew that I ought not to be rude to her, that I had no reason to be rude, but I could not hit upon any other tone.

" 'Vasa, she's dying; Ivan Zakharievitch said so.'

Ivan Zakharievitch was the doctor—her doctor and adviser. 'Is he here?' I inquired, and all my hatred for her revived.

" 'Well, and what if she is?' I continued.

" 'Vasa, go to her. Ah! this is dreadful!' she sighed.

" 'Shall I go to her?' I asked myself. And I at once decided that it was my duty to go to her, that it was the correct thing to do in such cases; that when a husband kills his wife, as I had done, he is bound to go to her. If it is always done, I reasoned, then I suppose I must go. Yes, if it should prove needful—I said to myself, thinking of my intention to commit suicide—I shall have plenty of time to do it afterward; and I followed my wife's sister. 'Now I shall have to prepare for grimaces and phrases,' I said to myself; 'but I must not let them affect me.' 'Wait a moment,' I exclaimed to my sister-in-law; 'it is so stupid to go without boots; let me just draw on my slippers.' "

CHAPTER XXVIII
GOOD-BYE!

"STRANGE AS IT may seem, as I left my study and I passed through the familiar rooms, I once more conceived a hope that all this had not really taken place; but the pungent smell of the abominable drugs, of iodoform, of carbolic acid, overpowered me, and I knew that it was a dread reality.

"Passing along the corridor by the nursery, I saw Liza. She gazed at me with a terrified look in her eyes. I fancied all my five children were there, and were steadfastly looking at me. I went up to the door of *her* room, and the maid opened it and went out.

"The first thing that struck me was her light gray dress lying on the chair, all black with blood. She was in bed, in my bed, which was easier of access than her own, lying on pillows in a very sloping position, her knees upraised, her camisole unbuttoned. Something had been laid on the place where the wound was. A nauseous smell of iodoform pervaded the room. What impressed me in the first place, and more profoundly than anything else, was her swollen, bruised face, the eyes and part of the nose being of a bluish-black color—the effect of the blow I had struck her with my elbow when she was trying to hold me back. No trace of beauty was left, but instead of it I noticed something repulsive in her. I stopped at the threshold.

" 'Go up to her—go up to her!' exclaimed her sister.

" 'Yes, she probably wants to repent,' I thought. 'Shall I forgive her? Yes, as she is dying I suppose I may forgive her,' I decided within myself, striving to be magnanimous.

"I then went up close to her bedside. With difficulty she raised up her eyes to me, one of which was greatly bruised, and said, falteringly, stammering over the words, 'You have your way now; you have killed me;' and I observed on her face the expression which was struggling with physical pain for the mastery; in spite of the nearness of death it was that of the old, familiar, cold, animal hatred. 'The children—you—shall not—have; I will—not give—them—to you! She' (her sister)—'will take them.'

"As to that which was the most important point of all, for me—her guilt, her faithlessness—she did not consider it deserving of even a passing allusion.

" 'Yes, admire what you have done!' she exclaimed, slowly turning her eyes in the direction of the door and sobbing. On the threshold stood her sister with the children. 'Yes, see what you have done!'

"I looked at the children and then at her bruised, blue face, and for the first time I forgot myself, my rights, my pride; for the first time I saw in her a human being, and so frivolous and mean did everything appear that had wounded me, even my jealousy, and so grave, so fateful the thing that I had done, that I was ready to fall at her feet, take her hand in mine, and exclaim, 'Forgive me!' But I did not dare. She closed her eyes and remained silent, evidently too weak to speak. All at once her distorted face quivered, a frown passed over it, and she pushed me feebly away from her. 'Why has all this happened? Oh, why?' 'Forgive me!' I exclaimed. 'Forgiveness; all that is rubbish. Oh, if I could only keep from dying!' she ejaculated, raising herself up a little and fixing on me her eyes that gleamed with a feverish luster. 'You have worked your will. I hate you! Oh, ah!' she exclaimed, evidently frightened of something, as her mind began to wander. 'Kill me now, kill me; I'm not afraid. Only kill them all—kill him too. He's gone—he's gone!' The delirium continued to the end. She recognized no one. The same day at noon she passed away.

"Before this, at eight o'clock in the morning, I was taken to the police station and transferred from there to the prison, where I remained eleven months, awaiting my trial. It was there that I meditated upon myself and my past life, and succeeded in getting a true insight into its meaning. Three days afterward they took me over to the house—" He was going to say something more, but he could not muster strength enough to repress his sobs, and was obliged to stop. Making an effort, he continued:

"I only began to see things in their true light after I had looked upon her in her coffin." He sobbed again, but went on hurriedly: "It was only when I had gazed upon her dead face that I realized what I had done. I then felt and realized that it was I, I who killed her, that through my instrumentality it had come to pass that she who a little while before was living, moving, warm, was now still, wax-like, cold, and that this could be righted nowhere, never, by no one. He who has not experienced this is not capable of understanding. . . . Oh, oh, oh!" he ejaculated several times, and lapsed into silence.

We remained seated in silence for a long while, he sobbing and shivering opposite me. "Good-bye," he called out at last, and, turning his back to me, lay down on the seat, covering himself up with his plaid.

When we came to the station where I had to get out—it was eight o'clock in the morning—I went up to where he lay, to take leave of him. Whether he was asleep, or only pretended to be asleep, I could not tell, but he did not move. I touched him with my hand. He uncovered himself, and then I saw that he was not sleeping. "Good-bye," I exclaimed, holding out my hand to him. He stretched out his hand and smiled, almost imperceptibly, but so piteously that I was moved almost to tears.

"Yes, good-bye," he said, employing as his last adieu to me the same words with which he had finished the story of his life.